THE PAGES

THE
PAGES

A novel

MURRAY BAIL

OTHER PRESS   NEW YORK

Other Press edition 2010

Production Editor: *Yvonne E. Cárdenas*
Book design: *Simon M. Sullivan*

This book was set in 10.75pt Galliard by Alpha Design &
Composition of Pittsfield, NH.

10 9 8 7 6 5 4 3 2 1

Library of Congress Cataloging-in-Publication Data

Bail, Murray, 1941–
The pages / Murray Bail. – Other Press ed.
p. cm.
ISBN 978-1-59051-353-8 (pbk. original with flaps) – ISBN 978-
1-59051-381-1 (e-book)   1. Philosophers–Fiction.
2. Psychoanalysis and philosophy–Fiction.   3. New South
Wales–Fiction.   4. Australia–Fiction.   I. Title.
PR9619.3.B25P34 2010
823'.914–dc22   2010016756

THE PAGES

1

AT DAWN—what a word: the beginning of the world all over again—the two women set out from Sydney in a small car, as other people were slowly going about their tasks, or at least beginning to stir, producing a series of overlapping movements and stoppages, awakenings and false dawns, framed by the glass of the car.

They were city women. Comfortably seated and warm they were hoping to experience the unexpected, an event or a person, preferably person, to enter and alter their lives. There is a certain optimism behind all travel. The passenger, who wore a chunky necklace like pebbles made out of beer bottles, had never been over the mountains before. And she was forty-three. Directions had been given in biro, on a page torn out of an exercise book. It would take all day getting there. Over the mountains, into the interior, in the backblocks of western New South Wales, which in the end is towards the sun.

At an earlier time, perspiring travelers found no other way but to hack a path through the jungle or the dry bush. Very common image. Now on the long wide road called Parramatta, the obstacles consisted of nouns, adjectives and flags, and flashing lights in the shape of arrows, the many different interruptions of color and promises, honestly, the hard work of selling jutting into the road itself, cluttering and distracting the mind. Traffic kept stopping, starting: you'd think by now they could synchronize the lights.

The woman behind the wheel preserved a high, elbowy method of steering and changing gears, more like a series of nudges and prods, which can only be described as feminine. It was her way in general. It suggested refinement: everything's temporary, take the provisional position, in stages.

Erica Hazelhurst had a calm face, pale lips. In profile she had an elegant nose which became more ordinary as she turned. She lived alone.

A few years younger, her passenger had a slightly large head, which most people missed, because it was obscured by a restless, self-absorbed energy. She was a woman always losing something, leaving it on a table, or on a chair, or in the back of a taxi, as if dropping clues to herself for someone to follow . . . sunglasses, a glove, keys, books, purse, and, once, her virginity. Now she had one foot on the seat and head bent, painting her nails. As she concentrated she was at the same time describing a man they both knew. She turned to her fingernails. With rapid precision she reeled off his recent behavior, and proceeded to go through his lesser-known qualities, some of them good qualities, which only gave greater credence to his evasive and careless qualities. In rapidity and sureness of touch they could have been paragraphs snipped out of some sort of manual, a manual of Types, various case histories pointing in a clinical style to Inevitable Behavior, et cetera.

Finished, she ruthlessly inspected her nails. She didn't appear to notice they were bitten down. Now she wanted something else to concentrate on, some other situation—a person—and Erica, waiting for the attention to turn to her, adopted a very smooth expression.

It was often like this. Instead of ease of familiarity they enacted a kind of hectic casualness, more like a demonstration of familiarity, which required no response. And months would pass until one of them called on impulse, no particular reason, or when one was having difficulties of an unspecified kind; then they would pick up, as if they had left each other only the day before.

Erica glanced at her friend's hair—reddish, open to experiment. Her own was short, determined, academic. And she noted too with some admiration the blouse which appeared to be casually chosen, of faded silk, here and there traces of embroidery, and buttons undone, where shadow offered the ample promise of softness.

"I would make a gloomy wife," she felt like saying, but frowned instead.

She immediately wondered why she had had the thought in the first place—was it a true one? And why would it appear as out of character to people nearby? Concentrating on the driving, she saw it was hardly a thought at all, more one of those non-thoughts, those that come in from every direction, interfering with possible clear-thoughts.

Sudden rain—hit the metal car—glittering sunlight, rain again.

They were on top of the mountains, the road rising and falling and turning this way and that, which had their heads leaning one way, then the other, passing tearooms, railway station, shops selling old kettles and cane furniture, corner hotels and hotels set back, whitegoods, petrol, pink paintwork, pies, newsagent. A woman stepped out and waved to someone, not them. Presbyterian church there converted into a carpet emporium.

Sophie—the passenger—now examined herself in a compact mirror, paying close attention to her teeth.

"So much for the Blue Mountains. I haven't seen a single instance of blue."

Below, on the right, a purple sunlit plain appeared as if unfurled on a butcher's calendar. Patches of mist erased the red roof of a homestead and an entire paddock of merino sheep. It had something to do with ground and air temperature. To Erica, anything that suggested incompletion or hazy thoughts made her impatient—the years of training. Had she, by trying all her life to banish woolly thinking, become harsh—was she a hard woman?

The question had been coming upon her in unexpected places, such as the bathroom, stepping out of the shower, at the supermarket, reaching out for the tomatoes, in class recently when she was in the middle of a medieval sentence—without warning, the oddest times. The frequency of it implied a concern deep-seated. This was not about to go away. In the bathroom, naked, just herself, she could only glance at her shape in the mirror. Can a woman be strong and clear without turning hard? Hardness—not something we want to think about in a woman. Erica almost opened her mouth to ask Sophie. Had she—now intent on steering this efficient Japanese car—had she become a cold-hearted, off-putting woman? "Do you think I've developed a hard side?"

Erica Hazelhurst had a lovely, rounded body, patterned from her mother's, pale, with hand-shaped hips, the two vertical halves not quite symmetrical. She wore flat shoes. Erica came from a family that didn't believe in a person drawing attention to themselves. Her mother and father, and her six uncles and thin-as-a-rake aunts, and their neighbors also behind hedges in the short hot street in Adelaide, made a point of keeping thoughts to themselves. To talk was to wave attention to yourself. Better to clam up. As for talking about feelings—this was a really difficult area, without solid foundation, more trouble than it was worth; better to keep the lid on feelings. The prevailing stoicism might have come straight from the sticks, the dry unyielding country. It puts the squeeze on words. The place hadn't been feminized yet. Still, it generated its own set of decencies. There was an underlying honesty in Erica's family—in relation to economics, and towards all other people. And no one would dream of complaining about the plainness of circumstances.

Her father had a shop in one of the granite buildings on King William Street, third floor, between a stamp dealer and a milliner. The first time Erica saw him behind the counter she hardly recognized him, her own father. It made her twist her legs and look away. To protect his cuffs, her father wore a green cardigan she'd never seen before, and elastic bands on his sleeves. These he put on as soon as he arrived at work. Fitted to her father's eye was the protruding magnifying thing. It would stay there all day. With practiced movement he levered open the back of a silver Longines, exposing the insides which shivered like an oyster. When it came to payment, Victor Hazelhurst never actually replied to the customer but searched around for a scrap of paper and scribbled a figure and pushed it forward.

Erica was waiting at the bus stop for her father to come home. She held on to his thumb, and began talking. After a few steps he made an unexpected noise, not exactly a word, and slipped out of her grip. People came forward, some kneeling tried pushing his chin and cheeks. The sun was shining. Even the bitumen road was harshly lit. For a long time Erica didn't know what or how to think about anything much. She believed she stopped thinking. Corrugated iron church there looked more like a shearing shed. A brown horse stood against the entrance, out of the wind.

Now more than anything Erica wanted to make sense of her life. It can be a strain trying to understand brief moments, the fleeting registrations, as well as what appeared as long and solid, or at least constant; always returning to herself, how and where (and why) she fitted in. Erica said to herself she was a separate individual, a live being who happened to be a woman. She tried to go on from there. No one else on earth was like her, not even in appearance. It was amazing how her sister born of the same parents barely a year before didn't think or speak or look like her at all—especially now they were in their forties. And over the years this person, herself, Erica Hazelhurst, had encountered endless experiences, each one of them supplying unequal additions and alterations to her original self—it included experience of words—a multilayering which increased still further her distance from other people, other women. These experiences passed through her, as did time, and in contemplation and possible measure of this she drew near to what has been called "thinking about thinking." The trouble was: she was excluding everybody else.

2

How ANYONE can believe that Sydney could produce in its own backyard a philosopher of world significance or even minor significance shows how little understanding there is of the conditions required for philosophical thought.

Sydney of course is one of the nicest places under the sun. The location, location. A young settlement, brightly lit. It has come late to just about everything, and enjoyed both the advantages and disadvantages of that. The first arrivals were conveniently composed of thieves, forgers and unmarried mothers, accompanied by unshaven soldiers and tragic magistrates, the shopkeepers, brewers and road-builders, the brick-makers, midwives, followed by farmers and farmhands and others (the horse-dealers, publicans, four-eyed tailors, stunted fettlers), all hoping for a fresh start. They could hardly be expected to pursue philosophical interests— most of them couldn't write their own names. For the first fifty years there was only a handful of books in the entire country. Other missing ingredients were slavery, or an imbalance of religion and superstition in daily life, or else a collective stammering of the self, a general mood of darkness and obscurity, and some would include a cold climate, all of which have in earlier times turned people to philosophy for answers. By the time Sydney passed through and built upon its original settlement and began standing on its own two feet, philosophers, if there were any, found hardly any problems left for them to tackle. The important philosophical questions had more or less been settled. The remaining questions were paltry; they could all fit onto a pinhead. People in Sydney still interested in philosophy were reduced to commenting on the work of others, and in their isolation became world authorities on figures at the margins, such as Charles Peirce or the terrifying Joseph de Maistre.

In the late nineteen-seventies there used to be a man who lived in a boarding house in Glebe, a thin short-sighted man, with an exceptionally wide mouth. Most days he could be seen in the park at Black Wattle Bay, lolling about and squinting up at the clouds for hours at a stretch. When he wasn't doing that he'd be seated on the park bench, sharpening a blue pencil with a pocketknife, as if he was refining an original idea. He wasn't known to rattle on about anything, let alone thoughts of a philosophical nature. He kept his thoughts to himself. Children were occasionally caught throwing stones at him. He may have been one of those who'd lost their marbles in the war. And yet—or rather because of all this—people said he was a philosopher! What a country. Greengrocers and policemen were fond of giving a tolerant wink in his direction, "the philosopher," or "our very own philosopher."

At the very word "philosophy" people in Sydney run away in droves, reach for the revolver; they look down at their shoes, they smile indulgently; they go blank.

It is different in other places; Berlin, Copenhagen, Vienna come to mind. There, philosophy is not in the awkward, remote background, but in the foreground of everyday life. These are places where the philosopher has his rightful position, that is, on a pedestal. It is common in those old cities to find a philosopher's image cast in bronze and his most difficult propositions being discussed over breakfast, and certainly every other evening on the radio.

Meanwhile, Sydney never bothered itself with philosophical questions; as a consequence, philosophers are nowhere to be seen.

Such an absence normally would leave a hollow center, an entire group of people living without the benefit of long sentences—foundation sentences; yet we can now see how the lack of interest in one field encouraged a rushing across into an adjacent field, the way passengers crowd to one side of a ship when a harbor comes into view.

Psychology, and its vine-like offshoot, psychoanalysis.

In Sydney it's hard to bump into anyone who isn't in analysis, or has been, or is about to be.

From being the most unphilosophical city in the world, Sydney has become the most psychological city in the world.

Rows of terrace houses in the inner suburbs, and rooms in small office blocks close to medical centers, have been fitted out with the heavy curtains and the chair and the couch in duplication of the cavelike atmosphere first tried and found to yield interesting results in Vienna, on the other side of the world. In the long summer months on the footpaths, when the windows of these rooms are raised like so many open mouths, a murmuring hum can be heard, blending into one, each and every word and sentence circling around the self, nothing else. In early evening, women doing well in big business, earning heaps, hurry away from it all for the regular appointment. And they enjoy it—the endless sentence. Who knows what sacrifices they have endured

and confusions vaguely felt—all for their work? Others—
perhaps soldered to their father's hip, or baffled by the broken marriage—drop everything at three or four to make it
there. An excavation through words. It can be hard work.
And these patients are the articulate ones. Emerging after
fifty minutes on the dot they can be seen hurrying along the
footpath in a return to ordinary life, the everyday in all its
complexities, its apparent breadth, its incompletions, some
wearing an exalted expression, while fumbling for the keys
to the car.

What is going on here? The skies are blue, forever
cloudless—is that it? A great emptiness sending people
back to themselves. Now that the city is up and running,
no longer a country town, there's been a transference from
the landscape and its old hardships to the self? Various re-
pressions are said to be hidden away, "frozen anger" is one
of the terms used. They say it is a matter of gradually lifting
the layers, to find the original self, where there might be
recognition, which then allows a suggestion of hope.

It has become the age of the self; confessions in public all over the place, the spillage of the "I," and in private,
in a quietly structured manner (the therapist has replaced
the priest). And who is doing this talk? Not ill, at least not
seriously, the self-obsessed personalities have a concentrated, almost technical interest in the self, as if they were
specimens. Interest in others tends to be perfunctory, impatient, showy. It is they who have a natural attraction to
analysis, where again they can dwell solely on themselves,

the problematical "I," and, since this is the very source of their difficulties in the first place, there is a real danger of psychoanalysis not uncovering, but giving shape to, and confirming, a person's self-obsession. Eight, ten years in analysis is not uncommon. In Sydney parents have been sending their own children, not yet in their teens, into psychoanalysis—ironing out the unformed mind before the unevenness of everyday life could give proportion or self-correction.

Years spent murmuring the endless circling sentence, while the analyst remains almost, though not quite, hidden.

A philosopher would not allow this; but when needed there were none.

3

IT HAD BEEN Erica's idea to bring a thermos of tea. Along with the scarf and the coat with deep pockets—it's what you did when you left the city in a car. If she owned a traveling rug she would have thrown it onto the back seat too.

"As well," she said without turning her head, "I have a slice of ginger cake."

"Sometimes I wish I had your practical mind," Sophie gave a comfortable stretch. "It would make my life that much easier. Although, kindly look at me: I shouldn't be having a single calorie of anything."

It took a while to find a suitable spot, a matter of avoiding ditches and slopes and gates. On the one hand they didn't want an open space, where they'd be the only visible things in it, and yet too many trees close to the road gave them no space at all. Sophie said it was worse than buying clothes. They could have gone on for hours, never quite satisfied, until they both agreed on a single white gum tree and, although obviously not perfect, Erica braked hard, and skidded to stop near it.

At intervals a car passed and enveloped them in a system of metallic rubber rattling, vibrations.

Erica sat with the door open, holding the cup in both hands; she had her feet on the ground. Opposite was an old wooden farmhouse surrounded by dozens of rusting agricultural implements which appeared as gigantic, disabled insects. She had looked up and gazed at them. Under the Brittle Gum, Sophie's Italian ankle boots made a racket on the strips of dry bark littering the ground, for in new surroundings she liked to pace backwards and forwards.

Following Sophie's restlessness, Erica tried to imagine her stillness and patience, hour after hour, in her work. How could she do it? Only a person with a certain psychological necessity could submit.

Sophie had stopped moving. "We must be in the country. Here comes a man on a horse, behind you."

Erica could have reached out and touched it. It was a solid living mass, dark tan and glossy, here and there quivering, as it trod daintily. Jogging ahead was the man's kelpie, tongue hanging out, as if searching for water.

With all the space in the world, out in the wide open country, the man and his brown horse had come between the car and Sophie, two women, who were being crowded out. Peevishly, Erica decided he could have used the other side of the road.

The horse and rider stopped. Affecting a laborious style the man dismounted and came towards them, the women looking up at him.

As soon as the hat came off he looked ordinary. Vertical lines on his forehead and running down from his eyes traced the nation's crows, creekbeds, the salt plain, and tightened his mouth. His green shirt was stained, the pocket where he kept his smokes falling apart.

Indicating with his hat he said, "You won't be getting far on that one."

Sophie slipped into a little girl's voice, without being quite aware of it. If it was meant to make the stranger stronger it made this one crouch further over the tire. Erica watched. Could they at least hold something or pass a spanner? Not very talkative. Already he had jacked up the back and with fat fingers fiddled with the nuts, hardly a fumble. It was a strain squatting on his haunches, two women looking at him from behind. He cleared his throat. "They call the tree you're standing under the widowmaker. A branch is liable to land on the head."

What's he telling us that for?

"Then it's curtains," he said wiping his hands on his trousers.

Sophie was reaching out to the horse. "What do you call him? He's not going to bite, is he?" This particular man she was approaching through his horse; it was as if Erica, her friend, wasn't there. Veins were bulging on his neck as he tightened the last of the wheel nuts, which allowed him to get moving and not say another word.

4

ERICA WOULD always wonder why she was chosen. Of the seven in the department others had stronger qualifications, and all but one lived alone, as she did, unmarried. (The solitary life was known to strengthen clarity of thought; Schopenhauer, Nietzsche, Kierkegaard, Spinoza, Simone Weil—and anyway who would live with those sorts of people?—and don't forget Diogenes.)

She knocked and went into L.K.'s office. This was Professor L. K. Thursk of the pullover and bulky shoes, whose long-awaited study of Georges Sorel had become something of a myth—who swiveled side-on, as she entered, his hands pointing under his chin, an Indian prince wondering whether to give salaams. He was another one who had developed a hierarchy of throat-clearings, in his case necessary in the struggle to express even the most modest thoughts, for much of what composed the world was unsayable. He was like a plumber who had lost his tools. Erica though saw it more as a sort of fussy drapery from the bachelor life.

If she didn't want to do this, she didn't have to. From the beginning L.K. made that very clear. However, "It doesn't hurt if now and then a university reaches out into ordinary life, and on these occasions it is unusual for Philosophy to be called upon." Clearing the throat. "In fact, I can't think of another instance."

Along one side of the window an edge of sandstone showed, weathered and worn smooth by the never-ending revision of ideas, and a glimpse too of lawn, watered by a hissing and clicking metallic insect. Cloistered. The transplanted idea of the kind of aura necessary for a seat of learning. Erica wondered whether a fresh, angular philosophical method could ever be realized here. Time slowed at that moment; it became a honeyed substance. The room was slightly humid. The good professor would happily have waited more or less all day for an answer.

The following week she went into the Trustee Company, on Bridge Street.

It was a foyer which displayed at set intervals facsimiles of parrots and black cockatoos by the artist G. J. Broinowski, and a photo in brown frame of the building, c. 1906. At some stage the offices had undergone a fortune in wainscoting and woodstain. To carry out the instructions of the deceased demanded an atmosphere of quiet purpose, where even a judicious echo played its part.

The solicitor was Mr. Mannix. A large man, he had loose hanging cheeks, and pursed lips from the many years of putting words in parentheses.

People sitting across the desk from Mannix, where Erica sat, had been singled out and their personalities assigned clear, material value. Assumptions were confirmed, or just as often given sharp correction. Mannix watched as favorite sons or nephews or the proverbial stepdaughter shook their heads in disbelief and became angry, silently cursing or looking up at the ceiling, some leaning back and laughing their heads off, as if he wasn't there, others abruptly getting to their feet and at a later date (to be determined) returning with their own solicitors decked out in identical broad-striped shirts and the somber suit to see if the will could be contested. There was happiness too. An unexpected windfall gave pleasure. It could strengthen memories. A confirmation. Mannix enjoyed seeing people appreciated in a useful way. Over the years a habit had formed of resting both hands on the desk, near the box of tissues, allowing his wedding ring and gold cufflinks to show.

Now he surveyed Erica Hazelhurst. No lipstick. With its slightly pronounced jaw her face gave off a studied calm. He had an aunt in Melbourne who was like her—very intelligent. Erica wore a faded cardigan the color of boiled rhubarb, which splayed over her hips, and speckled green slacks.

"I have known the Antill family for as long as I have been working here. When I say I know them, I've managed in these thirty-odd years to meet just one of them, and then for less than five minutes. But that's all right. Not a problem. The Antills are an old pastoral family. They can do what they like. Cliff Antill conducted his business through the post. It was said of Cliff he was afraid to open his mouth in case a fly flew in. All I can say is, there must be a heck of a lot of folk in this country going about not talking.

"He had racehorses. There was a photo from Flemington in the paper once, years ago, and I was surprised to see a thin man holding a champagne glass. I'd always imagined, I don't know why, a big fellow, sturdy. She—that was Mrs.—she was known for her hats. Her family made their money out of inventing a new shoe polish. I gather she preferred her apartment at the Astor to the sheep station out in the mulga. Mrs. Antill left endowments to music and the State Library. I managed to dissuade her from leaving any monies to theater companies."

The filing cabinet, the venetians from the nineteen-fifties, the exceptional neatness of the desk, its broad glossy surface, the photo there of wife and kids, and Mannix's motionlessness as indicated by his stationary cufflinks, his purple lips producing the only movement, like a little hidden engine, as they formed the steady horizontal arrangement of words—all these things transferred attention onto Erica. She tried to imagine how he would be as a father to daughters. If only he'd fiddled with a paper clip, perhaps just twisting one out of shape.

"When Mr. Cliff and Mrs. passed away, as we all do eventually, the property passed in equal shares to the children. These children are Wesley, the eldest—come to him later—Roger, and the daughter Lindsey, with an *e*. They lived together in harmony, and worked the place without much trouble. Wesley has now died. In his will, he has bequeathed his share to the brother and sister."

The phone rang and Mannix answered: "Not now."

"I met Wesley. It was in this office. He made an appointment and sat in the chair you're in now. It was fourteen years ago. I had no idea what he wanted. An Antill had never come into this building before, not one of them. He sat there a good minute or two before he realized he still had his hat on his head, so he took it off without a word. He had a fair bit of white hair. He didn't crack a smile throughout. I remember thinking: this is not a happy man. He'd just got back from Europe, perhaps that was it. You could see by his general manner and clothing he'd been away."

From his trousers, Mannix drew out a large handkerchief, blew his nose and put it back in his pocket.

"He says to me, 'Mr. Mannix, I'd like to change my name. How do I go about it?'

"Wesley would have been early thirties then. I said of course it can be done, we can do that. We can do anything here. But why? I reminded him the name Antill wasn't any old name, but a name with a history, a name stuffed to the gills with squatter connotations. It is not to be dismissed easily. I felt I could say that. I said, I didn't particularly enjoy my own name—what sort of person do you conjure up when you see 'Mannix'?—but I wouldn't dream of changing it."

Here Mannix leaned back in his chair.

"He listened politely, then he said *Antill* was not the right name for a philosopher. A philosopher, he said, words to this effect, had to have a name appropriate to his work—his labors, he used that word. *Wesley* he didn't mind. It wasn't perfect, but it wouldn't be a burden. If necessary he could just use the initial. *Antill* was the problem. It was light, that was the problem as he saw it. He said there can be no such thing as "light" philosophy. It was a contradiction. He said it more than once—a contradiction. To be a philosopher was impossible enough without being lumbered with an inappropriate surname. I must have had a silly look on my face. He said to me, "You don't know what I'm talking about." He was explaining that to come up with a meaningful philosophy was one thing. The difficult part was to convince others of it. Everything had to be in place, I remember him saying. To succeed it was necessary to rid himself of all disadvantages, and that included his name. A philosopher had to begin with authority, in every way. That's roughly what he said, words to that effect.

"I think he was winding himself up. Nothing came of it."

It was enough to trigger in Mannix memories of other clients and their bizarre instructions. "I had someone else who died," he wanted to say, "who left his neighbor a pair of gates. He didn't want them."

His advice was to keep everything simple.

"I say to people: hang on, spare a thought for the executor! Not to mention the added expense."

An informal tone had entered his voice and manner which Erica found disappointing.

Mannix gave her a glance, "Goodness me, on the scale of difficulty I have known people worse off than Wesley Antill. One of our clients is called Mound—Mr. Leon Mound. How about that? We also have a Murray Pineless on the books. And let's be perfectly frank. If this was about photography and not philosophy there wouldn't have been any fuss. So now we have this small difficulty."

He adjusted one of his cuffs.

"According to his brother and sister, Wesley Antill was in fact a philosopher. That's all he did when he went back to live on the property—write his philosophical work. Very generously, it strikes me, his brother and his sister didn't mind. Not at all. They had a very high opinion of Wesley. To them, their eldest brother was a genius. Or perhaps they thought he could have been. For years they worked the property and gave him the free time, and the space, and all the rest of it, to write. And that is what he did all day. And what was the result of all this? There is a provision in his will. It is clear enough. It asks that his philosophy be published and the costs be borne by his estate. Is this possible? Is he a genius in philosophy? We have no idea. That's where you come in. The university tells me you are an expert in this field. We would like you to examine this 'philosophy,' or whatever it is he's put on paper, and supply an opinion."

"Yes," Erica nodded. She almost went on, "I can identify with Wesley Antill. The difficulty, my God. I am very interested in this. And it will be something to look forward to—the drive, getting there, everything."

Mannix was in a hurry now.

"Roger Antill and his sister are expecting you." He went back to his desk and found the handwritten map. "It should be pleasant this time of the year." He shook her hand. "Not too hot, not too cold."

5

SOPHIE HAD her arms folded. All it took was a flat and dusty tire to interrupt her flow, enough to have her pondering what else might be in store, as if she and she alone had been singled out for obstacles, uncertainties. Very little was needed to bump Sophie Perloff off course. A person she didn't know might say something careless, incorrect or deliberately outlandish, and Sophie would begin pondering, looking into herself and away.

Dead something on the side of the road. Two small dams were laid out in the shape of artists' palettes.

In her work Sophie was supposed to remain neutral, be the conduit. Instead of a couch in the office she used a *chaise longue*, draped with a kelim—a splash of geometric individualism. Here the patient was forced to lie neither horizontal nor upright. Some found it necessary to grip the sides which resulted, one afternoon, in a thin woman's wedding ring slipping off and rolling along the floor. Otherwise, discomfort was not something they noticed. "The only men I have on the books are ex-priests," she explained to Erica. Some patients fell into the category of super-articulate (an aspect of their intensity). When the session came to an end they looked disappointed. Others faltered even as they were absorbed in talking about themselves. Some began sobbing and couldn't stop, disliking, as they saw it, their own unlikeability. It was not unusual for a patient to pay good money every week to stretch out perfectly still or fidget slightly on the recalcitrant chaise longue, their fingertips reaching to the floor, and not open their mouths until the last few minutes when there'd be a flood of recollections, of experiences they evidently groped around for in the dark, and now held up, and turned over, and recognized as vital evidence. Lying there and not saying anything, just a twitch of the fingers, and Sophie seated somewhere behind as an invisible prompter, a person could begin to see how they were unpleasant and unattractive, and how this had affected others; and, although it was a source of unhappiness, they felt happy being able to recognize and describe it, as if they were carrying out their own treatment of themselves. Traffic noises and the sound of birds came into the room, allowing Sophie's mind to wander.

It required patience of an extreme kind to listen over and over to the words of others. In many cases the subject and the way of talking were only slightly different from all the others. A lot of what was said screamed out for intervention. Instead of answering a question with a question, Sophie sometimes—unexpectedly—gave an answer, a harsh one. Her own opinion, if you don't mind! She found her own self mysterious. A lot of obscurity there. On occasions her own monologue took over. Of course it is not supposed to happen. It was precise, colorful, multilayered, and absorbing to Sophie, but having to lie there listening to such an articulate outpouring was not what the fumbling patient had come for.

Recently, Sophie had slept with a patient—one of the ex-priests. She waved away the risk. "Can I say something, Erica? These men are fascinating, believe me. They are double-men. They have an entirely different take on things."

From the beginning to the end she enjoyed the process of meeting, then sleeping with, a man. Astride him, these chosen men, she could look down on her opaque self, and spread a flooding generosity, and for a moment, forgetfulness. Otherwise, Sophie found intimacy difficult. She couldn't sufficiently involve herself. She could not reach out. And she enjoyed experiencing the inevitable weakness in men, of seeing the effect she had on them, from the moment she turned her special attention on them.

She preferred the company of men to women. It didn't stop her from having women friends. Recognizing her behavior, they looked on it kindly. As for the men, they understood at a glance she would not be trouble. Many of her affairs were with married men; and these men had made a calculation. Whatever they had murmured to Sophie, they would never bring themselves to leave their wives for her, not even the most crabby, fading wives. It wasn't the way it worked. Sophie knew that. And with a married man any ideas of permanency could always be postponed—by the week, by the month, whenever. Now, though, something felt missing. At forty-three, Sophie was facing discomfort, uncertainty in the form of vague emptiness. The smallest thing could throw her off balance—not much, but enough to make her pensive. Erica saw this in the folded arms.

A recurring problem for Sophie was her father (though he didn't see any problem). To Sophie, he was in front of her and above and to the side. The solid shape of her father. Just by being there he could unsettle her. Something he said. Or when he said nothing at all. It was her father up to his tricks again. Immediately she would call Erica to discuss. She had to talk to somebody. Erica was always there. She seemed to be sympathetic. Sometimes she asked a question. If she did, Sophie would continue without answering. "And do you know, I think he's basically oblivious?" Then there was the stepmother. Sophie could hardly be in the same room as that woman; and this didn't concern her father at all. "Well, I am sorry, but I find that perplexing and very hurtful"—Sophie speaking to Erica.

Perloff, Harold G.—where does that come from? Stopping and U-turning it went back in a faint line to a town in one of those tangled, landlocked countries in Eastern Europe, where it became dark at four in the afternoon. It might explain his mysterious limp—story there. Hemmed-in countries produce all manner of limps and missing limbs in their men. Along with a certain ironic superiority, his limp gave Harold Perloff a way of sitting in a chair, ankles crossed, and sipping an espresso from tiny gold-rimmed cups, with his little finger sticking out. Here was a large round bald head, noticeable for its warts and protuberances, bobbing up and down like one of those floating World War Two mines that wreaked havoc in the Mediterranean. The bow tie sometimes fitted on Fridays resembled a propeller below the waterline. He was playful. He was also implacable; when his daughter thought of him, which was often, he had his eyes on her.

At Bankstown, the enormous rusty roof of Perloff's factory had grown into a local landmark: with an immigrant's pride he liked to joke you could see it (the rust) from an aeroplane coming in. H. G. Perloff & Co. manufactured hard hats of reinforced plastic for working men, smaller helmets in glossy blue, red or yellow for children. As Harold told it, to anyone who'd listen, it was good and proper to protect the all-important heads of construction workers, oil-rig operators, coal miners and the like; but he had real doubts about legislation which had small boys and girls strapping on one of his products the moment they stepped outside, for it diminished the thrill of being on your own in the playground, or of balancing on a bicycle. A law promoting softness, a suburban law—it would produce problems further down the track—his very words. He had a view on everything. Still, Harold Perloff understood the decency of making something and being paid for it, and churned out the hard hats by the thousands, selling them into Asia, and places like Fiji and Papua New Guinea.

"I can tell you, the girl was never short of a word," he said to Erica, early on. "Now I believe she is being punished by having to sit still all day and forced to listen."

Although he had experience enough of banks to be dismissive of the well-educated person, he was pleased with his daughter's diplomas, her quickness, the way she dressed in bold colors. Look at the cut. She was expensive. He didn't mind that in a woman. But he could only shake his head at how she spent her day, listening, according to him, to people moaning; she certainly wasn't out there making anything with her hands.

When months passed and Erica hadn't seen her friend it usually meant Sophie had become involved with someone again. Across Macleay Street one morning they waved to each other, and Sophie phoned the next day.

"I cannot think of a single irritating factor about him. You know—how it doesn't take long before you begin to think up reasons and excuses?"

Married with four kids, he was a lecturer in Medical Ethics. At least once a day they spoke to each other; this time Sophie was determined. They had even managed a weekend away together. According to Sophie, he was calm, and steadiness was something she valued more and more. Then she turned to the man's intellect and achievements. "He's always reading philosophy. I've been meaning to tell you. He keeps up with the subject. It is presumably essential for his type of work."

Later, she told Erica he had a valuable collection of antique corkscrews, and he wore socks and underpants always bought from the same shop in W1, London, which had a miniature hedge out the front.

Erica never got to meet him. With little warning he too went the way of the others. When Sophie unexpectedly dropped in on a Sunday morning, wanting to talk, she began weeping.

They were in the kitchen.

"What you need," Erica said, slicing a lemon, "is to get away, and therefore remove your thoughts, as it were, from what has happened. Does that make sense?"

Unusually for Erica, she said it firmly. At the same time she was aware of the liquid glitter squeezed between her redbrick building and the next, and the horizontal orange of a container ship sliding past.

Tuesday she was leaving.

Sophie laughed, and blew her nose.

Nothing much happens in my life, Erica wanted to say.

My movements are minimal; and it doesn't always feel right to me.

And now, a long way west of Sydney and the tires making a reassuring humming, Sophie sat up and decided to sing, Erica joining in.

Tearjerkers from Verdi and Puccini were tried out, but soon they switched to the less arduous "It's a Long Way to Tipperary" and other chestnuts, "Let It Be" and "Up on the Roof."

After that Sophie tried the radio—nothing but static. How could anyone live out here? To Sophie, the large paddocks represented a mind emptied of variety, of life itself. Except in the occasional towns they had hardly seen anything on two legs. But the great homesteads set back and surrounded by trees were not visible from the road.

They were bumping about along a reddish track.

Sophie had a handkerchief pressed to her nose. "I've never been enamored of dust. I'm going to start sneezing in a second."

Erica was beginning to wonder why she had agreed to the task, which required a long drive, shaking the car to pieces, and every minute leaving further behind what was familiar. She had been restless. She needed some sort of change. As they went on, the names of the places had become more and more remote; Merriwagga, Goolgowi. Where did they come from, and what did they mean? Now as they turned south on a stretch of bitumen the two women began talking again, in anticipation.

"Do you have any idea where we are?"

Erica had stopped to consult the handwritten map. "What time is it?"

"Is that handwriting his? Let me see."

Erica got going again. "He has a sister. I believe I told you that."

Both looked at their watches. It was only four, but they didn't want to be searching for the homestead in the dark.

6

AND THE AIR had taken on the golden furriness as they drove up the avenue lined with imported poplars (as if all the staff of the big house had been summoned and stood in welcome), driving slowly to avoid colliding with stray animals—dogs, sheep, et cetera, for all they knew.

There was an unexpected garden—the greenery, roses—and to the side a flagpole, machinery, shearers' quarters, the corrugated tank on stilts—representing labor, self-reliance—which threw shadows angular and out of kilter across the gravel, implying the presence, surely, of patterns and complexities to be traversed. The shadow of the house itself folded out flat, as if it was being wrapped in dark brown paper. There was a wide veranda and outline of windows, a screen door; a woman bent over two barking dogs on long chains, looked up.

Sophie turned to Erica, "Did you say I was coming too?"

As Erica stepped out of the car, the woman came forward. She apologized for the dogs—"harmless, just ravenous." It was good of them to come out all this way. We—that's her brother—were grateful.

Then she stood still, as if she was trying to remember something. She doesn't have many visitors, Erica concluded; and immediately worried they were overdressed—two smart women, fronting up from the city.

Expecting them, Lindsey Antill had applied a slash of lipstick, the quick dark slash tilting her mouth, enough for Sophie to wonder whether she really wanted them there.

Before they could object she took their bags; they traversed the shadows, passed the dogs now smiling, their tongues hanging out, and entered the Antill homestead, a large house of high ceilings and many rooms. Wherever they stepped it creaked like a ship.

Off the central corridor, their bedrooms each had a fireplace and a small desk by the window which reached to the floor.

"My brother will be in later."

Erica sat on the edge of the bed. Taking off her watch, she lay down—heaved a sigh. Parts of the road they had been on appeared, and the petulant lips of the solicitor in Sydney, and the worn-out man on the horse. Briefly she considered her pictorial admiration of horses. As usual, her mother's face was blurry. Was Sophie the right person to be traveling with? Better—easier—alone? Erica wondered if she had brought the right clothes. By now the brother should have turned up. First thing in the morning she would sit down and begin the task. It was a privilege to be allowed into the mind of another person, the life work of another. She was curious to see what he had thought, what he had found. Already she respected his effort. It would have been difficult to sustain across pages, the many years, the isolation, the heat, perhaps the silence.

7

THE DINING room had a fine English table, silver candlesticks, and heavy knives and forks set for four. Under the table was a Persian carpet of soft faded pattern as if coated in dust. Otherwise the floorboards were bare, dark jarrah. It was a long room. Maroon-striped wallpaper decorated one side, and the stripes were very nearly obliterated by rows of official photo-finishes from Randwick, Warwick Farm, Flemington, Caulfield, Eagle Farm—Australian suburbs, endowed with a more concentrated purpose. To the untrained eye the outstretched horses strung out in a line all looked the same; their names were printed underneath, back to the one bringing up the rear. The rest of the room was empty, except for a shotgun leaning in the corner.

This matter-of-fact masculinity was modified by Lindsey coming in wearing a dark velvet dress and earrings.

It took Sophie by surprise. "And I of course didn't think to bring anything to wear. All I brought," she swung around to Erica, "is virtually what I have on. In other words, *nothing.*"

Lindsey Antill's smile widened and remained wide. "Our father and his iron laws, dressing every night for dinner being one. It's not uncommon on the older properties. Our father took it to extremes. Even in the middle of summer he wouldn't dream of coming in and sitting down without a coat and tie."

Mention of the father and Sophie would rush to collaborate. After all, her own situation was exasperating too, and cried out for description.

"Oh, that's interesting. Tell me more. Did you find you could talk to him, I mean easily? Were you close to your father? What I have noticed is they assume in their little heads they are close enough, while we—the poor confused, misunderstood daughters—may not think so at all. Don't you find? I know with my own, who's still alive, touch wood, he's completely impenetrable! Do I understand him? I'm his only daughter, if you please. He keeps me at arm's length, in every sense, which makes me want to scream. Normal intimacy is foreign to him. He resembles a lump of granite."

But then she smiled as she remembered how easily he made her laugh.

Lindsey had a rectangular face, a pink shoebox with worn edges, and therefore appeared to be a practical, sensible woman.

"Fathers are interested in things we are not," she said. "The way he was hard on my brothers, Wesley especially. He did it without so much as blinking."

"Women like us who have a father-problem have difficulties with men."

"Do I have a father-problem?" Lindsey frowned. "I don't think so."

Brushing a speck of dust off her hip Sophie gave the impression she was perhaps more knowledgeable in this particular area, at least when it came to the behavior of men.

Half-listening to them, Erica, with no warning, had a dizzy spell. She almost keeled over. Although she sat down, she felt like limping.

Sophie and Lindsey were smiling at something they each said.

"I am sorry," Erica got to her feet. "I think I need to lie down."

Sophie came forward. "You look like you've seen a ghost." She touched Erica's forehead: it didn't tell her much.

All Erica wanted to do was lie down. She'd go to bed. In the country, people got up early.

The bedroom was quiet.

At crucial moments in her life, Erica paused; it had become something of a habit. If she happened to be advancing along a promising path, such as a line of abstract thought, she would, at the moment of possible resolution, hesitate, and remain in one spot, like a car waiting at the lights—just to be sure—an afraidness of continuing, of embracing result. If she took the next step it might all unravel, perhaps. Instead of taking one more step she took a step back. With people too, a similar story. At the moment when all the instincts nudged and whispered, continue, go forward to this person, Erica, while remaining friendly enough, held back—reluctant, just then, to allow her true feelings. It would mean opening up—to what exactly? It had happened with a number of men. By withholding she remained in an uneven state, and some days she felt incomplete.

And now, inside a strange house which made her feel small, where for many years her designated subject, Wesley Antill, had lived hidden away, a philosopher unknown to the rest of the world, she was expected—and she had agreed!—to rifle through his papers, his life-thoughts, and cast a judgment on them, that is, on him. What she had imagined back in Sydney to be a privilege was swirling with presumption. No wonder she felt sick at the thought.

The house was so large Erica wondered what she was doing there. It was as if she was already asleep.

For a philosophy to be possible today it would have to begin afresh—"begin with nothing." Go back to the beginning where there was no thinking, no philosophy, and from there begin again. Otherwise what was the point?

• • •

The light angling in from one of the windows varnished the floorboards, lit up the Tasmania-shaped stain on the wallpaper and concentrated a magnesium triangle across Erica's pillow, splitting her troubled face. At the same time a crowd of large birds she was told were white cockatoos set up a hectic overlapping racket outside.

When she opened her eyes again Lindsey was holding out a cup of tea and buttered toast.

"Don't for a moment think you've got to get up. You're not in a mad rush, are you?"

"I don't know what's got into me." Lifting an arm took an effort. "What time is it?" And Erica immediately worried that her voice sounded frail—or not frail enough.

As for Lindsey, a childhood of sunlight, tank water and calling out across paddocks had given her an outdoor voice, steady and clear, capable of distance, and to Erica it came as no surprise later to learn she once had vague ambitions to take over from where Melba had left off. Resting back on the pillows Erica examined one of Lindsey's eyes, then searched her face for traces, if any, of suffering, kindness, cleverness, disappointment, serenity. She knew nothing about this woman bending over whose face was rectangular and hair could have been cut with kitchen scissors.

"This is Wesley's bedroom. You're in his bed."

As Lindsey went on, Erica noticed the tan rubber band tying her hair, its simple suggestion of modesty. At the same time it worried her that most people she met soon became of little interest to her.

"Next door is where he had his piano. It's still there, under wraps. He'd sit and play for hours on end. Honky-tonk, that type of thing." Lindsey tossed her hair back. "It wasn't as bad as it sounds. At least there wasn't any static, which is what you get out here when you turn on the wireless. He said the piano was necessary to calm his thoughts, to settle himself. When he'd come in exhausted from his work he'd spark up after a few minutes playing. Wesley was the only one of us who could play a musical instrument. Basically he was a city man—the tall buildings. It took me a while to realize. He liked the bright lights. He did not really have an agricultural calling. He didn't take the slightest interest, not that we minded."

If only Erica wasn't feeling so feeble. Now instead of turning over questions of a philosophical kind she was finding herself picking up the slightest scraps of information on Wesley Antill's personality. Perched on the end of the bed, his sister now busily gazing out the window still hadn't said where he actually did his work.

"He took us by surprise when he came back here to live— the way he straight off began decorating his room with fancy chairs, sofas, some statues, silk curtains—you name it—it cost an arm and a leg. He had some idea in his head of the perfect environment. Anything that could help him in his chosen work. I don't know how he could make sense of the problems he was trying to solve. Way over my head."

Lindsey rubbed her eye. "It wasn't long before he threw it all out, the cushions, the lot, and just had a card table, a kitchen chair, no books, not one, and nothing on the walls. I called it the 'piano room.' He called it his 'simple room.'

"A woman came to stay with him once. She was from Sydney. I wasn't sure about her. She had a nice figure, and she knew it. Perhaps that was it. After about a week she left."

Listening to Lindsey talking about her invisible brother, Erica felt her energy return and found herself nodding at the bits and pieces on him, though she held back even in anticipation from what remained ready and waiting for her, his lifework.

Later in the morning, she decided to get up.

Sophie called out from her room. Seated naked in a small chair she was removing her nail polish; her body, exaggeratedly soft and pale, overwhelmed the chair. It made Erica consider the smallness of her own body. "What is a comparison?" had been the subject of one of her earliest papers (took an early things-in-themselves line; well-received).

"And you are feeling?" Without looking up Sophie went on, "I'm not sure I enjoy staying in someone else's house. What to make of that woman? I'm talking about Lindsey. She cultivates a sort of privacy, which I assume encourages us to try to look at her. Do you know what I mean? I'm not sure what she thinks of the two of us. What do you think?"

Finished with her nails, she smiled at Erica.

Sophie wanted always to understand the other person, every person she met. She liked nothing better than trying to fathom a person's behavior. She waded in. It was what she was good at. Unable to stop, she would first try to establish the source of the behavior, and by so doing she could for a moment put her own self to one side; at least it seemed that way to her.

"Guess what? The brother didn't turn up. You don't suppose he's run away from us and is out there hiding behind a tree?"

Erica smiled. If anyone should be running away it was her. Through the window she saw a tall pale-gray eucalypt surrounded by a darker cluster of pines, elms, cedars. It pronounced a solitary, take-it-or-leave-it way of being. The simple strength of the tree: stand it alongside the lack of statement, on her part. For a moment—before looking away—Erica saw herself as resolute only in a few minor things.

Sophie, she professed a low opinion of nature. "Basically, it is merely visual," she had been heard to say. "It just happens to be there, and that's it."

8

TRAVELERS AND strangers to all parts of Australia, especially away from the coast, can expect wonderful hospitality. The country has its faults, as any country does, but lack of hospitality is certainly not one of them. Only when hospitality is little more than an excessive informality, when an entire nation breaks into premature smiling and all-teeth, small-talk mode—which betrays an absence of philosophical foundations—does it appear as nothing more than an awkward type of lightness.

The more isolated and hostile the terrain, the more authentic the hospitality. In their falsity the travelers are made to feel at home. Desert people are renowned for sharing with strangers their last handful of dates and puddle of used coffee, often without saying a word. There is a courtesy here—without naivety. The world is inhospitable; the cold earth. Assist another person if encountered on its surface. The instinct is a basic one. In modern times it can be as minor as changing someone's flat tire by the side of the road. In a poor farm or village in Spain or somewhere it is common for a crust of bread and a lump of cheese to be wrapped in cloth and given to the traveler about to continue the journey. It is unsmiling hospitality. Other places are known to share their women with travelers.

At first glance you would think that the psychoanalytical person would understand hospitality, and be hospitable, whilst the philosophical person would remain distant to the point of turning away. The opposite happens to be the case. The psychoanalytical person plumps up the pillows and leaves it at that. To extend hospitality to another person subdivides aspects of their difficult, hidden self. And any suggestions of a food offering acting as a language are brushed aside: for it could only reduce the amount of language available to describe their own attention-requiring state of mind.

But then it could hardly be said the philosophers have set a cracking pace in generosity to strangers either. Almost to a man they practice in their daily lives a specific remoteness, a behavior verging on abstraction. Et cetera, et cetera. Oh, yes.

9

INSTEAD OF learning the fine art of wool-classing, Wesley had thought he might try something entirely different, such as science or languages at one of the universities. His father had other ideas. A push, which is eventually necessary between father and son, turned into a full-blown shove, and Wesley watched as his father, still reading the riot act, tripped and fell on his knees, kicking up a puff of dust. A scuffle near the veranda steps, Lindsey in a short skirt looking on. This was at the beginning of 1978.

By ten o'clock, not-so-young Wesley was on the train to Sydney, where he camped in his mother's apartment at the Astor. He soon realized he couldn't stay there. It was the powdered humidity, mirrors wherever you turned, the bathroom with its array of milky jars, bottles in the shape of hearts, tweezers and pencils, the miniature soaps from the south of France, little things, potpourri, the embroidered footstools—and his mother, the docile tea-drinker, long-fingered, a woman of taste, interested and yet not really— enough to have him step out after less than a week and find somewhere else.

The first apartment he saw was good enough. Typical of the buildings around Kings Cross it had a chrome-plated bolt of lightning decorating the glass doors, and a maroon carpet of floral pattern which darkened the foyer and continued into the lift. It was strange living in a tall building where so many other people lived—all those nearby lives, attended by the water and gas pipes and the electrical wires. Wesley's apartment on the fourth floor faced Macleay Street. A thin man with out-of-control black eyebrows, which gave him an untidy bachelor look, claimed to be the oldest resident, and made it his job to latch on to any new tenant, to help them "acclimatize," as he put it. He was known as Joseph. No abbreviation was possible. With Wesley he went around and pointed out the fuse boxes and the location of the rubbish bins; along the way he kept noticing things which reminded him of certain tenants and their exasperating behavior, and he went on complaining, shaking his head and so on, as he led Wesley onto the roof to show him the clothesline, raising his voice as he stepped over a young woman in a bikini lying on a towel.

People in the building came and went at all hours, and looking down from his window Wesley could see figures moving along Macleay Street, stopping now and then to talk. Where he came from, in the country, there was no movement after dark—nothing. By eight fifteen, everybody was asleep and loudly snoring. In the city, people couldn't sleep; and they talked more. Always someone, somewhere. Much of the talk was in the realm of small courtesies, although a man could often be seen arguing on the footpath to convince another to his line of thinking.

As for his own talkability, the endless paddocks and the creaking tin roofs had passed through him and left behind a teeth-sucking way of speaking/smiling. It suggested some sort of face-in-shadow reserve; but soon enough he joined in giving the standard nod and "Good morning!" to people in the building. Straw blonde about fifty-plus applied lipstick in the lift. She was the one who always asked him the time, yet didn't appear interested in the answer. Most mornings he had bacon and eggs at a café next to the Sicilian barber's. It was one of the side streets that form the misshapen asterisk, Kings Cross. He bought his cigarettes at a place that sold complicated mechanical ashtrays, the genuine Havana corona. He was twenty-two. Of course he liked the idea of smoking and looking thoughtful. Along the streets were spaces into which were fitted cramped enterprises, where figures bent over needle and thread, while others nearby did their best to resurrect wrinkled tan shoes, sandals and ankle boots, so reproducing the craftsman's atmosphere, not much different from the Middle Ages — one bloke still held tacks between his lips, as he cut leather and hammered. Others there on Darlinghurst Road had tired expressions as they cut pizzas into bleeding triangles which drooped over plates, day and night, like Dalí watches. Bottle shops, money changers, the fluorescent optimism of the all-night newsagent. Strip joints—"nite spots," they're advertised as—had a door opening onto stairs going up to nowhere, to darkness and pounding repetitious music, a spruiker or two on the footpath pointing up the stairs. To kill time or just being polite they listened halfheartedly to tarts bitching about the other girls. A stripper in a short coat looking cold and hungry running across the street to her next venue. Opposite the fountain, a butcher sold basic cuts and Australian sausages, unaware of the shifting demographics; Wesley noticed the way this gangling slack-lipped countryman sat down to his lunch at the back of the shop, tucking into two freshly fried lamb chops with liver, no vegetables. Pawnshops are drawn to the intersections, variety in all its messiness, no more surprising than the banks in there too, adopting a patient, resigned air, at least architecturally.

Street people spotted Wesley as a yokel, not only for his red ears and premature crow's feet, and the tan boots—only missing item being the hat—but also his wide-open gaze of one who had never before seen at close quarters eye-sliding men and women, jittery, and yet matter-of-fact types, flaunting themselves to make a quid—and the wear and tear it takes out on the eye, mouth, skin and sympathies in general. In the first week his wallet had gone. But this was a man earlier on Bayswater Road who saw a twenty-dollar note on the footpath and kept walking. Even back then he could hardly be bothered bending down—or seen to be stooping for anything.

At night he was a large slow fish with bulging eyes passing through the channels, changing mind, turning

back, taking in and digesting the many different movements between people, and the people themselves, their
expressions, temptations. In fact, the world had turned its
details in his direction; every little thing seemed to wait
in bright, clear light for his inspection. Edge of building, one eye bigger than the other, pigeons unafraid of
that fat woman. He felt like squatting down to examine
the very small and ordinary. Early in the morning, streets
were watered and along the gutters flowed bus tickets,
dry leaves, dead matches and toothpicks, cigarette butts,
torn notes, trimmings from fingernails, hair—all manner
of leftovers, discarded things. And as he kept seeing each
day something fresh on the street, he felt he was gaining
experience, or at least complexity, even though it was only
observation.

To have her boy within reach his mother had a telephone
installed in his apartment. And it became more or less established Thursday nights were set aside for her, his mother. If
other people were invited she'd phone and suggest he wear
a necktie; otherwise, it would be pasta or Thai takeaway
from trays, not saying much. A daughter might have been
better, but Mrs. Antill and Lindsey didn't get on.

Early on she inquired, "What did you do last night?"

"I went to a brothel, on Darlinghurst Road."

"Oh, that's nice. What was she like?"

"Blonde."

"I suppose she would have a nice figure."

"I think all she wanted was for me to make her laugh."

As for what his mother did all day in the city in amongst its verticals and congesting horizontals he could only wonder. To hear her women friends, she was incredibly, determinedly active, and—news to him—a bridge player at state championship level.

Whenever his father turned up he stayed at the Australia Club. It was a few minutes from the Astor—same street. After finishing his business or attending the races Cliff Antill went back to the property without looking in on his wife. And when after almost a year Wesley and his father eventually spoke again it was in the dining room of the club, where the oil paintings were benign and the lunch specialty was the steak-and-kidney pie.

Because there was no point going over their argument, and Wesley showed no interest in the horses, his father looked into the distance as if he was back on one of his paddocks, and talked about his stamp collection. There were collectors and there were philatelists, explained his father who had plump, weather-beaten fingers. And there is a difference. He was a philatelist. Look at the near-completion of his collection: among its treasures, the blue first kangaroo, 1912. All a man needs is a preoccupation, preferably involving classification. Later, as Wesley walked home by the water at Woolloomooloo, he saw how philately was a solitary pleasure which centered, unusually, not on the specimens secured in rows, but in the contemplation of those that were *missing*. Now there's a strange pleasure. And he could see his father sitting in his office at the homestead—could go for weeks without a word—identifying from his swivel chair the gap in the pattern of his life. His wife as a rare postage stamp! A figure of theatrical design who had to be handled with tweezers; for the moment unattainable, out of reach.

"Have you found your feet?" his father managed to ask as he bent into a taxi, not turning around. "More or less," he would have said at that early stage.

At one of the Thursday dinners Wesley found himself seated next to Virginia Kentridge, a friend of his mother's. Instead of talking he fiddled with his knife and fork, and considered the farm shed with its hard dirt floor, and on the bench the gray metal cabinet, which held in drawers, at different levels, screws and nails of various sizes; always interesting pulling them out and having a look, even if you didn't want anything. Under the bench old bottles, sheets of tin, lengths of wood.

"What are you smiling at?" woman, in black, cut in from the left. "You're thinking about some poor girl?"

A small tanned woman, Virginia Kentridge had a thin neck with prominent sinews sweeping up from her shoulders like a Moreton Bay Fig, enough to stretch her credibility, for when activated, which was often, they gave a neurotic force to any ideas she may have had. And this neck—those sinews—also suggested emotional adventure, just below the surface.

Wesley's mother had told him about her.

To commiserate he said, "Your husband couldn't have been so old."

What actually happened? (Why think, let alone ask? Why was he talking?)

"He was with his poxy girlfriend," Mrs. Kentridge smiled. "A clear day, a perfectly straight road, and he was driving. The rest I leave up to you."

"Was she killed too?"

The widow shrugged. In broad daylight at any given moment there was always somewhere a head-on collision taking place, especially on the road to Cooma. There were so many solid trees in Australia. Far better to lean forward, which she did, allowing him to glimpse the softness of her neglected breasts.

The following night he spent at her house. Photos of the husband in silver frames were still on the shelves—a man entirely frank with the camera, nothing to hide. Stacks of hair, the strong wiry stuff, and in silver eruption above his teeth like a burst water main. By looking straight at the camera he was looking straight at her.

Until Virginia Kentridge, Wesley had fumbled around with the willing experimenters from the nearby towns—on the slippery seats of locally made cars, he was the awkward skater on pale-green ice. But this energetic woman who exercised a tennis player's sinews in many parts of her body was only a few years younger than his own mother. No sooner had he begun that night to linger in her bed than she placed an extreme, restless importance on his feelings for her, and became different, making herself singular to him. So specific was the change, he wondered whether it could be true. He didn't know that her anxiety was close to momentary happiness.

Mrs. Kentridge reached out to him. Oddly she complained he wasn't talking to her, yet when he did she looked away and fidgeted, sometimes getting up and putting something in a slightly different position, as if she wasn't interested.

Taking him shopping gave her pleasure. Shirts in boxes, woolen tie, diamond socks, a rust-brown herringbone jacket, gave form to the idea she had of him. He appeared more sure of himself than he actually was.

By now he no longer looked like a hick, which therefore you would think an improvement, but it caught the eye of his cosmopolitan mother—narrowed her glance, well-practiced at isolating a situation. And when the happy and bold Mrs. Virginia Kentridge insisted they go to hear a Russian pianist giving one and only one recital at the Opera House, which happened to be a Thursday evening, Wesley casually went along and didn't go to his mother's or get around to telling her.

The following morning she phoned early.

"What have you been doing? I sat here and I added two and two together. The poor thing, that's all I can say. We don't know what's the matter with Virginia. Why does she have to carry on the way she does? The fresh widow. She's trouble. Listen to your mother. Are you listening?

I know women like her. You have to be careful." The bridge club at Double Bay and the tennis group were full of them—and not only widows and divorcees—tanned, gaunt, large-eyed, fierce women. "Find someone younger. They're around. I saw some lovely young things on the street yesterday."

The way she spoke rapidly as if to herself, his mother didn't sound like a mother at all; to his surprise he saw the younger, single part was still there.

Now she said, "I've got to go now. I'm going out."

He took ferries too, cream and green ones looking like nineteen-fifties kitchen cabinets, and bus and train journeys— to Parramatta, more than once—stopping at the regular intervals—across to the North Shore—as far as Palm Beach. He preferred the buses where he could gaze at the haphazard mess of streets and the people on them, and glance at the passengers as they made their way to seats near him. Old ladies wearing coats on hot days and women clumsy with children he helped on or off. He began to wonder what he was doing with himself.

On a noisy night the students next door invited him in, where he entered the source of the music, steady, blurry, blood-pumping, and the rising and falling laughter and shouting. He was dragged in. Men and women his age stood in the one spot and made pronouncements from what they had learnt that very day in the lecture hall. It was not possible to remain silent; Wesley was expected to agree or not.

A woman he had seen once before brushed past him and went into the kitchen.

She put her hands over her ears. "I don't know where all these people have come from. And I have this terrible headache."

He filled a glass of water, and sat across the table.

"Where do you fit in?" she looked up. "What's your story?"

"Last time I saw you," he decided, "was up on the roof. I think I saw you there."

"He only thinks it was me . . ."

Sturdy thighs, Wesley remembered. Lying facedown, reading a book.

She said, "Up there, I'm all by myself. All I can hear is the traffic—and the pigeons. I hate pigeons. There's nothing attractive about them. They're both disgusting and boring."

This was Rosie Steig, close up—a broad forehead, narrow chin, severe eyes, messy black hair to her shoulders. She was studying Old Norse and psychology, among other things. Wesley explained where he came from. Because she had asked, he described his sister. Even with a headache she listened carefully. His mother and father he mentioned with a shrug. Describing his interest in impressions and movement, he realized he didn't make sense, and sounded almost mournful when he said he didn't know what to make of anything much.

And the kitchen became crowded. Although they were in her place, she asked over the noise if they could go next door to his place. There, still talking on his secondhand sofa of muddy roses, he allowed his left arm with its restless fingers and a Swiss watch strapped on, to lengthen towards the first port of call, her shoulder. At the very moment his fingertips touched, he stopped. She seemed to be waiting—but you never can tell.

Later, lying next to her, conscious of the welcome of a woman's body, again Wesley Antill decided to pause, decided to remain separate. He concentrated on the smallest gaps between them—not to remain faithful to the memory of Mrs. Kentridge, who he was still seeing, but to experience the difficulty, the austerity of resistance. Was it celibacy? It was close, but not really.

From then an apparent naturalness flowed between them; a pleasant ordinariness, none of the complications.

A few weeks after the party she suggested one afternoon they go up on the roof. It was too "stuffy" inside. Chatting away at the bedroom door, she bent forward to let her breasts fall into the floral bikini he had last seen on the roof.

To his sister he wrote, "My neighbor next door is like you. I'm trying to work out why exactly. (When I know I'll let you know.) Is about your size. Don't screw your nose up! Name is Rosie. She tells me there's no problem attending lectures at the university. All I do is tag along as if I'm a student too, which of course I am."

Rosie Steig took him to other parties, where he looked on as she and her friends discussed politics, and names and ideas Wesley had never heard of. He left early, and didn't mind when he heard Rosie arrive next door with another man. It was Rosie who first led him through the gates of Sydney University and into the lecture hall. With Wesley in tow, she liked to arrive late, and take a seat in the front, where she would begin brushing her black hair. To Wesley the descending tiers of seats gave the impression he was stepping down into a volcano, or some sort of excavation where, instead of eruptions, a small vertical figure stood at the microphone and spoke with quiet reasonableness, trying to make sense of it all. It was here that Wesley first heard the main theories of psychology and psychoanalysis, which had been transported in book parcels all the way from Vienna, Zurich, London.

Whenever he looked up one of Rosie's friends waved at him using her little finger.

Nothing before had produced in him such keen anticipation. The process itself of arriving and choosing the best position for learning, then to sit down and wait for the lecturer to arrive, watching and waiting as the papers were shifted, sometimes just a page of notes, before the mouth opened and pronounced the first words. It hardly mattered what the subject was. Theory and information unfolded as one. In this it resembled the way Mrs. Kentridge undressed in stages, proud to reveal her nakedness to him—who flew into a rage when he happened to tell her this.

He attended as many lectures as possible. And so he acquired broad knowledge of the histories of the significant parts of the world—really, a history of congestions. Even a bit of Australia was touched upon; he traversed the Spanish lake; listened in on linguistics, the Romance languages; Greeks, the myths; political theory; the Russian novels; utopias; various anthropological subjects. It required study. He filled almost to overflowing the emptiness of his childhood and youth with density—with gray matter. Even at breakfast he had his nose in a book. For eight months every Thursday morning an analysis of a Shakespeare play was given by one man. Beginning with the first, each play was examined in detail, until every play was done. A one-man show. Among the talents of this popular lecturer was the ability to read parts, switching from a la-di-da voice of a king to a high, clearly enunciated woman's whether mother, queen, witch, loyal daughter.

After the first year, Wesley concentrated on subjects he was interested in—discarding, for example, colonial and postcolonial fiction, yes, and the slide shows that represented the history of European painting and architecture—and law, and Old Norse—until, after some hesitation, he turned to philosophy, a subject he had avoided, where he immediately caught the attention of one lecturer.

10

IT WAS A puzzle to Lindsey that these two women showed no interest in walking around the property. Visitors from the city, for instance, couldn't resist looking into the shearing shed. The impulse is common to associate an unfamiliar composition with a familiar one; why, some people squint up at the clouds and spot the windswept features of Beethoven or Karl Marx, and even Queen Victoria. The bare ground between the homestead and the scattered sheds had the appearance of a piazza in a dusty, out-of-the-way village in southern Italy. Dog there scratching himself. But these women were happy to sit all day in the kitchen, nibbling biscuits. The brainy one, who was supposed to know all there was to know about philosophy, fiddled with a spoon. She hadn't been out in the sun, and was not given to saying much. She was somewhere else. Lindsey saw again her attractive matter-of-factness; and in recognizing it, although hardly knowing her, she imagined they could like each other.

Meanwhile, the gold-jangling arm and hand movements of her friend, Sophie, expanded the kitchen, which was large to begin with, as she explained how she ended up coming on this trip, for by talking about it she was talking to herself. It had been a telephonic nightmare canceling her appointments. For some time now she had been turning away new clients, as they were called. People, she said, had become desperate to talk. They talk virtually to anyone who will listen. You see them on television. It's a matter of have-to. It's themselves they want to talk about. As a qualified listener I do my best to guide them, Sophie told them. We pick up clues. Invariably what is said has been said by many others before, in slightly different form. It is certainly the age of anxieties. Many pressures today.

"As you know, Erica was coming here to work. Oblivious of this fact I had gone to see her. One of Erica's qualities is her subtlety. I had no idea she was coming out here. I was not in good shape. This man—I won't say who, in case he's a friend of yours—meant a huge amount to me. I mean, we were at ease together. As well, here's a man who made me laugh—me, of all people. I realized I was happy. Believe me, stacks of men are dull. They're all selfish, I know that." She turned to Erica. "And I have known you for how many years? Have you ever seen me with a man who has suited me better, and who has put up with my less attractive parts?

"Whatever. This ideal situation collapses. It sent me into a shocking spin. I wasn't prepared. I didn't know where to turn, what to think."

Erica stirred, "He was married." She also wanted to say she had never met the man.

"Yes, but it wasn't insurmountable. We were in the midst of discussing that very situation. I don't understand why he decided to finish with me. It must be something I've said or done. I'm trying to think. There was no warning. Do you know he sent me a letter?

"I am a discarded woman. In coming here I feel I've made the correct decision. I definitely needed my mind somewhere else."

Having heard this in the car, Erica allowed herself to gaze at the cream-enameled, industrial-strength wood stove. Pots and pans and kettles were larger out here.

"I am sorry," Lindsey said. And she was. A confusion now twisted Sophie's face as the two women looked on. Perhaps Lindsey should have touched her shoulder. A warm handful of life making a connection, a helping hand; it can sometimes make a difference.

To restore possession of herself, Sophie looked up and asked Lindsey about her two brothers.

Lindsey leaned over to pour the tea and wondered what she could say that would interest them.

"They were my brothers, yes. And they could hardly be more different. One day I would prefer Wesley, the next day it was Roger. The two of them and their opposite opinions on every subject under the sun, though they never really got into rows. I don't think Wesley could be bothered, Roger—he should be here in a minute—he has his practical side. He gets on with it. I suppose his common sense, which he has in spades, comes from being on the land. Wesley has been the more difficult one."

"And?" Sophie prompted. "Keep going."

"And what?"

"You were talking about difficult. Do you mean moody, habitually withdrawn?"

In the brown glaze of the teapot the table was reflected as a sphere, spoons and a fork clinging to the underside of the curve. Lindsey tried to think of anyone at all like her brother—especially when he came back after years away, his differences then. If Wesley had a difficult manner it was because he was constantly and unusually different.

"Going on and on about photography. He could not stand it. Just the sight of a person holding a camera was enough for him to cover his face or bend down to do up a shoelace. He'd only been back here a few weeks when he was accidentally photographed on the main street in town, and it appeared in the local paper, just the back of his head, but recognizable. It wasn't about him at all. He went berserk. The idea of being photographed made Wesley physically ill. His very words. I know you'll think there's vanity in that sort of carry-on. Who can make sense of our many foibles? These ideas, his hatred of photography being one, were necessary for his work. Don't ask me to explain. It made perfect sense to me. And Roger would agree."

"Can a photograph be as bad as all that?" Sophie sounded annoyed. In her apartment she had at least a dozen photos of herself, different stages of, arranged on sideboards and small tables.

Lindsey turned to Erica.

A photograph excited curiosity, because it wasn't true enough; a chemical image is at one remove from the original.

But Erica said, "Whatever helps in difficult work is what I say. I must admit, though, I would like to see a photo of him. Could a person tell you were brother and sister?"

"Wesley had biggish ears and they stuck out, not like mine, as you can see. He called them outlandish ears. He didn't like them one bit, until he came back here years later to live, and he convinced himself that his ears made their own separate contributions, as he put it, to the task he was involved in. A philosopher has to look the part, just like a farmer or a priest does. I think he's right, don't you think?"

"A phobia can begin with an earlier embarrassment. My mother," Sophie suddenly remembered, "she had exceptionally tiny ears and never went without earrings. I think I got my father's."

Erica felt herself separate—in thought, and almost bodily—from the two other women. Tomorrow morning after breakfast she'd embark on her appraisal. She'd open the door, enter the room where everything was still in its place. According to Lindsey, not a single piece of paper had been touched. Erica would sit at his desk. It was a problem—up to her to solve. With a careful anticipation she would reach out and pick up the page, and begin reading the first sentences of what he had to say, his life's work. "Let us think about gray, which means thinking about non-gray." Something along those lines. Or else a startling new theory of the emotions.

"I hope he gets run over by a truck!" Sophie was saying. "Him and his English shoes and socks, and his stupid fat wife at home. I'd like the worst things to happen to him in his life, for what he's done to me." Here she paused and shook her head. "Of course I don't mean that."

The sudden spilling out with hands and arms waving was accepted as normal by the other two women, the way a tropical island consisting of lush rounded hills, shadows and a single river produces its own weather, rain and wind to be soon followed by slanting sunlight.

At the end of the long driveway was a silver-painted mail-box cut from a petrol drum, and as they walked back to the house they appeared as three women advancing in a row, each with their own views of optimism. One sorted through the mail, the one in linen and raised heels talking to the smaller plainer one, who was glancing up at the tops of trees. The air was thick with the smell of sunlit grass, and like the heat which surrounds a railway line the earth made hot any bits of metal in touch with it, the fencing wire, gates, spanner in the dust, the corrugated iron sheds.

Lindsey said something and turned.

A light truck which had a flat tray where two tan sheep-dogs were balanced on tight legs had turned in from the road, and soon enough drew level.

"I've been to the funeral."

"Oh yes, that's where you were," said Lindsey.

This was the missing brother, Roger Antill, in cream shirt and tie. When introduced to the two women he some-how leaned his head and hat out of the window.

"Which one is the philosopher?"

In Erica's experience, men often resorted to mockery, which was sometimes enjoyable, often not. And it made still more complicated the problem of how to talk to another person, in this case a man. But he held an interested expression. And thinking they might have misunderstood he said, "I see you're going for a walk. I'll keep going."

Using her face, Sophie could produce many different compositions of herself. Now she leaned at a steep angle.

"Which one do you think it is?"

He looked at them again.

"I'd better leave that to the experts."

Erica wondered how the weather-worn face would look on a Sydney street. For all the asphalt hardness of the place she hadn't seen many, at least where she lived. And she applied a recent rule: a face weather-worn can appear more interesting than it actually is. (The monosyllabic horseman squatting to change their tire.) Roger Antill had a drought-cracked forehead. His hair was combed straight back in furrows, as if he carried around inside his head, even in the moonlight, the Idea of the ploughed paddock.

Then he tilted his hat with a finger.

11

As HE DEVELOPED ideas and opinions people were attracted to him. He became more and more himself, less and less like everybody else. For a while he was interested in so many subjects, as a consequence had developed so many theories and difficulties, some of them conflicting, it became necessary to sort through and test each one of them. Most he discarded.

Just about everything imagined is of no practical use. Of the many ideas, how many are put to "use"?

Almost by chance Antill sat in on the first lecture by Clive Renmark. It was said in the staffroom: "Renmark is not remarkable." He had a pedigree rare enough to excite envy. One Sunday afternoon in Cambridge, 1913, in amongst the deck chairs on a don's back lawn, Ludwig Wittgenstein had patted him on the head when he was a boy still in shorts, which was enough later to land him tenure in philosophy departments in England and North America, and finally at Sydney University.

Renmark went about in nothing but an open-necked shirt, even in the middle of winter, bringing inside to the lecture hall and the corridors the rude good health of the long walk, the heath, the stout walking stick, and all that. Wide open and crisply ironed, the shirt exposed a hungry look. Renmark had a gaunt throat. He was sixty-plus. And he was hungry—forever leaning towards something out of reach.

Here was Renmark at the lectern. Wesley Antill took his seat in the front row. By way of introduction . . . Philosophy was nothing less than a description of the impossible. If it was close to anything it was close to music. You had to be *porous* to allow it. Therefore, noble—it was a noble *enterprise*. He spoke of the "Everest of thinking, the pinnacle." Approximation, that's all you could expect. It was a climb—towards what exactly? "Forget the exactly," he said, glancing in Antill's direction. It is more in the realm of being "precise about imprecision." Other words he threw at them were "maps" and "mapping," and "blindness," "on all fours," "the candle flickering and almost going out," "stumbling about in the dark." A common candle, he told them—here Antill underlined—was closer to philosophy than electricity could ever be, the "spurious certainty" of the lightbulb. "What sort of *serious* light is that?"

Philosophy was a by-product of the Northern Hemisphere. Nothing much has happened down here. Why so? Dark forests, the cold, the old walls, the shadows of superstitions worrying the darkened lives, windows closed, all were pushed about by words which joined up into propositions to let in light, a little, a *dark light*. "Too much light is fatal for philosophical thought." But some light is necessary. To leave the dark room led by the faltering light of philosophy. It was the way out "to somewhere else."

After that, Renmark introduced the main Western philosophers by describing their lives. Without fail their stories were strangely interesting. He revealed how they managed to earn a living, and drew attention to the rare instances of a philosopher being married. It was up to the philosopher to become a *singular* person, he said more than once. Initially, some had been soldiers, or physicians, or tutors; there was the gardener in the monastery; others would remain disgruntled university workers or public servants; more than one went mad; suicides. With each lecture he summarized an individual's achievements, declaring this man, always a man, seemed to have found the answer, or perhaps half-pointed towards a possible answer. Running his tongue over his front teeth, nodding at the lectern, Renmark then proceeded to dismantle him, or rather his philosophy by introducing his successor. Each philosopher stirred another.

The Germans, he added mysteriously, were not always guilty.

Among the faces before him, Renmark had noticed Wesley Antill in the front row. While the others remained more or less motionless this one's head kept going up and down, from the lecturer to his notebook. He wrote more sentences at a faster rate than anybody else. To have at least one person hanging on your every word like a stenographer gave pleasure to Renmark, and he slowed his delivery, at one point pausing to blow his nose, and to look thoughtfully up at the ceiling, only to watch as Antill scribbled still more in the same time.

He never missed a lecture, and always had the same seat—front row, center aisle. Renmark noticed he was the first to get to his feet and leave when it was finished, no interest in coming up to him, as others did, with questions or to ear-bash him with their own obtuse arguments. At his age the regularity of Antill's habits was unusual; it was conservative. Out of respect, he had taken to wearing one of Mrs. Kentridge's expensive knitted ties, which didn't always match his bottle-green V-neck.

Stoicism, Cynics, the Thomists (the reasons behind these names). The foundations laid by the Ancients, their dialogues, the one who took poison, Logic, the endless difficulties of Ethics, to St. Augustine, for theology has to enter, and so forth, towards the Moderns; Renmark found himself more and more speaking directly to the one in the front, his most attentive listener, as if the rest of the seats were empty. If Antill noticed, he gave no sign. He listened with expressionless concentration, oblivious to any whisperings and movements around him.

On this morning, Renmark had left the Continentals and was progressing smoothly up the Thames towards the deepest English thinkers.

As always, Renmark had for breakfast yogurt and a green apple. He proceeded to explain language and falsehoods. There were theories of knowledge. How the empirical tradition formed. A Scottish philosopher was for a time tutor to a lunatic. Gathering up everything he knew, Renmark arranged it in reasonable order and gave it back to them—these students, now. The instability of sensations was an area he had become especially interested in. Speaking without notes, he was enjoying himself. What did it all mean?

Out of the corner of his eye he saw Antill pause and lower his pen. Still talking, Renmark looked at him openly. It was then Antill did the most startling thing of all. He began shaking his head at what was being said.

The following week Renmark took the rare step of leaving a note. He suggested Antill visit him in his office. Antill was seen to read it, but left before the lecture began. It didn't occur to Renmark that his most promising student was not really a student at all.

Those deep thinkers wearing the obligatory whiskers and who clearly practiced the austere life had a lasting effect on Antill. Before he encountered their example he had been one person; after, he was an entirely different person. "I was only half alive—or, not fully awake," he explained to Rosie, sounding more like Clive Renmark. "It was a before/after situation."

He would often wonder where this sudden all-powerful interest came from.

The true philosophers were possessed of an ambition to erect an intricate word-model of the world, an explanation, parallel to the real world. Antill looked up to them and then became more composed. Between each lecture he had studied further, reading everything available, and so began weeding out the philosophers he found incomprehensible, and others who were all too comprehensible. Models that simply didn't stack up. The dead words—accumulated, overlapped. Of no use, the way old battleships were left to rust. Later, he would describe it as wearing someone else's heavy coat. It was a matter of casting off. The few philosophers he allowed (Germans), he set about examining and dismantling—their letters, notebooks—the details of their lives—conversations, scraps—until without actually discarding he placed them in the back of his mind somewhere, for possible reference, along with the memory of Renmark, the open-necked moist-lipped messenger.

Two times they saw each other again, both on Darlinghurst Road.

Near the fountain one afternoon Antill was standing on one foot as an older woman smart in a black dress, low neckline, argued with him. She could have been his mother, except her unhappiness was specific. A bachelor, Renmark probably lived nearby. Months later, down the seedier end, Antill saw Renmark talking to a bottle-blonde, small, but with a large handbag. They were negotiating; and the lanky lecturer of philosophy followed her up some stairs. Although they never spoke, Antill felt a flood of affection for the determined shape of Clive Renmark going forward, always forward.

12

AFTER PARKING near the tank-stand the missing brother stepped out in front of the three women and proceeded to walk bowlegged to the veranda, a jockey too tall for the job, followed by his dogs.

Sophie and Erica saw just the back of him.

After being friendly to amble away twenty seconds later oblivious of them may have been the country manner; Erica imagined he was keen to take off his tie and get out of his suit.

"Please tell me," Sophie stopped in her tracks. "Did I say something wrong, or what?"

In her present state it was all too easy for her confidence to be thrown, the slightest thing could do it, which she normally would overcome by directing all her specialized energies onto another person, an onslaught of probings, suggestions, statements, questions posed but not expecting an answer.

Turning to Lindsey, she found her no longer there. Lindsey was at the tank bent over a metal watering can, and with simple calm movements she gave water to the roses, demonstrating there was nothing exceptional about her brother's behavior.

In the afternoon they each went in their separate directions. Erica placed a notebook and pen by the pillow, just in case, and lay on the bed. She waited.

From the distant rooms came faint creakings and a general muffledness which added to the strangeness of the house.

It was almost unbelievable that in this place one brother had been left alone for years and years—as long as it took—to construct a philosophy . . . and the younger brother went out and about in all weathers to manage the more than ten thousand merinos in dozens of different khaki paddocks, seeing to their salt and water, the miles of fencing, et cetera, the dipping and crutching, organizing the teams of perspiring shearers with their lists of demands, and so on. A rare sort of man not to have resentment. A respectful man. Erica closed her eyes. Aside from a certain anxiety, another reason for not rushing to examine Wesley Antill's written work was concern for Sophie. Her friend was reasonably calm, but Erica had noticed a tightening in voice and manner. Her movements had become rapid. With nothing to do and no one here so far properly to engage, Sophie was just as likely to announce she was returning to Sydney, "straight after breakfast." Spontaneity is Truth was one of Sophie's beliefs. For Erica it was of interest, possibly attractive, but of course had no philosophical merit, even if that wasn't the point.

Later in the afternoon, Erica went outside and strolled alongside the large house, keeping to the shaded sides. The full force of the wider silence combined naturally with the heat, and she felt it surrounding, swarming and entering her. Twice more she did the circuit. She asked herself if she was humble. She wanted to be humble.

Passing a window she heard a voice. It was Sophie talking intimately into the mobile. All she asked was that he listen to her for ten seconds, no more. "Listen!" It didn't matter that his wife was in the next room. "Stop it! Listen to me!"

She wanted an answer: was he missing her—at all? "I need to know, I want you to tell me."

But she wouldn't let him answer, even if he could, for she continued appealing, explaining, jumping in. Finally, "I don't know why I bothered." And hung up.

After waiting a little, Erica went back inside and wandered into the kitchen where Sophie was still talking, now to her father. She had swollen red eyes, but was smiling and gesticulating with one hand, explaining to him where she was. He'd be laughing his head off to hear his fancy daughter was such a distance from the streets of Sydney. She waved to Erica. Talking to her father, she concentrated. Very firmly she asked about his health and gave instructions not to drink so many espresso coffees. Making an elongated kissing sound, she said goodbye.

"I've had a terrible day," she turned to Erica.

They sat down at the enormous scrubbed table.

Speaking of her father, Sophie smiled. "He always says, 'How's my little girl?' I find I'm talking to him more than I used to. He's an unusual man. He likes women," she said to no one in particular.

Yes, Erica nodded to herself.

"He likes you," Sophie joined in the nodding. "I can tell. And he doesn't exactly have a history of rushing for the brainy ones."

Evidently she was thinking about her pushy stepmother who spent a fortune on hairstylists and eyebrow pencils and rejuvenating creams, French lingerie, a roomful of designer shoes, personal trainers, luncheons and a yapping poodle. Her father's casual slap-and-tickle tolerance of his younger (by seventeen years) wife irritated Sophie.

"I am sorry, but I don't get what he sees in that woman. Do you know he met her when she was modeling one of his yellow hard hats? Can you believe it?"

As Erica laughed she momentarily saw herself as a desiccated woman. And she was not meant to be, surely. Just as her small apartment with narrow kitchen was exceptionally tidy, her mind was neat and tidy. Her clothes too suggested a life simplified. Still, she was attractive to others, she had noticed. It was her alertness, in general. To those nearby, Sophie being one, she was a reliable presence. She had an attentive manner. At the same time she held herself slightly out of reach; Sophie didn't seem to notice.

Meanwhile, how in her own work to make something meaningful of the conflicting mass of impressions, propositions. Et cetera, et cetera. Daily. It was difficult—her chosen profession.

Sophie's father was a big man, a solid man. Every room became small.

Sophie had gone quiet, but now began talking about her earlier call.

Erica interrupted. "He's not worth it. Don't even bother."

To her own surprise she continued a series of dismissive motions with her hand. "From what you've said to me, nothing about him rings true. And, correct me if I'm wrong, isn't this a married man?"

None of these objections were of interest to Sophie.

"I could tell he was pleased to hear me, but he couldn't speak freely."

Lindsey came in. Glancing at their expressions, she put on the kettle.

"I managed to talk to him," Sophie reported. "He knows now I am still alive. And then I spoke to my father, who you'll meet one day, I hope. That's if you don't mind being chased around the table by an older man of obscure origins. Erica, am I not right?"

Without waiting for an answer she talked rapidly. "My father suffers from what is called in my circle . . . Never mind what it is called. He uses his eyes as very effective weapons. A watchful, patient man, at the same time energetic."

"Sounds all right to me." Lindsey sat down opposite. "These are my mother's cups. And I've yet to break one."

As Lindsey poured the tea she removed all expression from her face. "I didn't see much of my mother. She had a comfortable setup in Sydney. That's where she wanted to be. We would visit. It was nice. She had friends there. I was thinking only the other day I don't know the color of her eyes. Terrible, isn't it?"

"When you break a cup, you'll suddenly remember your mother's face." Erica then glanced at Sophie, who hadn't said a word.

"Did I make too many small demands on him?" Sophie broke in. "Did I correct him? I am sometimes guilty of that, I know. I lie awake thinking. The other thing is, I find myself listening in too much detail to everything a person says. It's a case of the professional life intruding into the personal—night follows day. I can't help it. Just as you," she said to Erica without looking, "can be too rigorously theoretical, which allows you not to participate in the life that's standing at your elbow."

Holding a cup, Lindsey took an interest in all this, or rather, in a woman nearby displaying loss of equilibrium. The usual reason—it had happened to her, two and a half years back. And now she couldn't help visualizing him, almost an enjoyment. Erica, still seated, didn't mind Sophie's comment on her life, or lack of. It had been said before. She was never comfortable with these conversations enjoyed by women—there was an endless ease to them.

How to avoid the looseness and ease of "I." Beware of hysteria.

Lindsey stood up. "Since the heat has been knocking us for six, I thought for tonight we'd have cold meat."

It had become darker, the birds were noisy, and now the lights were on. Wrapped around Sophie's neck was a crinkled silk scarf, which gave something of a head-wound atmosphere. Adding to the layer of determined bravery she wore a new perfume (can you wear perfume—philosophically?).

Erica admired Sophie's mood. She touched the scarf. "I would call that rhubarb."

Before she could quickly add, "It's my favorite color," small sounds such as words and Lindsey setting the table were deafened by a dark mass rushing across the sky towards them, gathering above the roof, where it paused, then cracked open, a thunderous splitting apart, echoing, and again closer, making them jump. The plates and windows rattled and some of the startled horses lined up on the wall fell. Simultaneously, lightning exposed them to windows, the way celebrities under siege in hotels are flash-photographed from the garden beds. By then it was raining. It was coming down. Tons of nails or wheat or gravel hitting the tin roof, pipes and gutters overflowing, while the thunder continued but moving away.

The women were laughing wildly, as if they were drenched. And it was Lindsey who threw her head back and closed her eyes, raised both arms and waggled her hips, making herself part of an action of nature. Although she was shouting, they had trouble hearing.

"Is this a rain dance, or a fertility dance? I can never be sure."

"You can always get rain," Sophie pointed out.

Unwinding the scarf she joined in, twirling it over her head, throwing her arms about. It was something older than music.

Erica smiled encouragement, and felt at one with these women, but couldn't step forward.

"We always could do with a drop of rain, but this is ridiculous."

Slightly flushed, Lindsey returned to the table. They still had to raise their voices.

Here Sophie noticed the cutlery set only for three.

"My brother sends his apologies," Lindsey said loud enough. "Because of the weather he's had to go out. I'm told he has some sort of girlfriend in town, but I don't think it's that. There can be flash flooding. He wouldn't want to lose any lambs."

By touching her nose Sophie somehow managed to see herself, without a mirror.

"I imagine your brother has a lot going on in his head. Everything is happening at once. We can say hello tomorrow, so long as we're not getting in the way."

"If you can get a dozen words out of him you'll be lucky."

"Because he spends too much time alone—outside?" Erica asked.

Out here—more than in the city—she could see how everything already existed without description. As well, she was never comfortable with the way words were attached to a given subject—such as a tree, or the heat, let alone feelings. Though Erica knew Sophie would object.

"Silence runs in the family," was Lindsey's explanation.

"Listen to her! You're not like that at all! If anyone's the shy, hiding-behind-the-bush type it's my friend here—" giving Erica a little shove.

"Wesley wasn't much of a talker either," said Lindsey.

The chair waiting for Roger Antill was beginning to irritate Erica. It drew attention to him—a matter of filling in the space, anticipating his voice and manner.

"I don't know why I'm so tired in the country."

By not turning up, he showed his indifference to them.

Lindsey lit a cigarette. "I'll make a cup of tea and we can sit in the lounge."

"This missing brother," Sophie said to Erica. "Have we frightened the horses or what?"

13

WHEN VENTURING into the interior, travelers are warned to take cans of drinking water and tinned food. Should the vehicle break down, wait for help. Do not leave the vehicle. In stony country, rocks can be used to form a message visible from the air: help or here! Every summer, horror stories come in of tourists from Scandinavia, Britain, Japan who became lost or bogged in sand, or suffered some sort of mechanical breakage, or ran out of fuel, and in the high temperatures they eventually died of thirst. A recent case was a couple from Korea, just married. Their bodies were found a long distance from each other. Some years ago a family of five from the Midlands perished one by one after becoming bogged in the Simpson Desert, South Australia.

They'd arrived in the country less than two months previ-ously. A young German in shorts, T-shirt and sunglasses rode off on a motorbike into the red sandhills, the heat and emptiness; waved goodbye, off into the sunset; he was never seen again. Talk about terra incognita!

In the far north, avoid swimming in the lagoons—crocodiles. This country also has the most dangerous spi-ders and snakes in the world. Every year reports tell of snakes accidentally trodden on claiming another victim.

Hot barren countries—alive with natural hazards—discourage the formation of long sentences, and encourage instead the laconic manner. The heat and the distances be-tween objects seem to drain the will to add words to what is already there. What exactly can be added? "Seeds falling on barren ground"—where do you think that well-polished saying came from?

It is the green smaller countries in the northern parts of the world, cold, dark, complex places, *local* places, with settled populations, where thoughts and sentences (where the printing press was invented!) have the hidden urge to continue, to make an addition, a correction, to take an ac-tive part in the layering. And not only producing a fertile ground for philosophical thought; it was of course an hys-terical landlocked country, of just that description, where psychoanalysis was born and spread.

It would appear that a cold climate assists in the pro-cess. The cold sharp air and the path alongside the rushing river.

14

UNACCUSTOMED TO silence, Erica had woken early. She brushed her hair, looked at herself and went down to the kitchen. Lindsey wasn't there. Roger Antill was spreading butter and apricot jam on a slab of burnt white toast. Next to his plate, like a small warm animal that followed him everywhere, was his khaki hat.

After smiling she said, "Is Lindsey not up yet?"

"She should be by now."

"I've been feeling quite spoilt. Lindsey's been serving me breakfast in bed."

"That'd be right."

Before realizing he was acknowledging his sister's kindness, Erica said firmly, "I think she's a kind woman."

To consider this, Roger Antill looked out the window. It allowed Erica to see again his straight combed hair and now, below his ear, the early morning razor snick.

"Kindness . . ." he was saying. "That's a thought I've never had before. She's my sister, I hardly think about her. We're both of us part of the furniture. We've been in the house the two of us here I don't know how many years."

Wasn't it Lindsey who had said her brother kept his thoughts to himself? There was nothing stopping him.

"I'm racking my brains trying to think of someone I'd call *kind*. Would you call yourself a kind person?"

Erica shook her head. Definitions of goodness, truth,

kindness—and their opposites—were best considered in philosophical terms, at arm's length. With resignation she saw how others took an interest in people more than in austere principles which over the centuries had been erected around people. There was this rush towards the subjective, which had—part of the attraction—no firm basis. If Sophie were at the table she would have tilted this attempt at conversation towards her methods, the psychoanalytical. By asking question after question she would reach him. She would then surround him.

As she got up to make tea, Erica spoke over her shoulder, "It bucketed down last night. You went out in it?" Erica poured his tea. "Milk?"

Facing this man with a reputation for wordlessness, Erica found herself talking more than usual. He was sitting there in his faded blue work-shirt sipping the tea the color of woodstain she'd made for him. He had his hand wrapped around the fine china cup the way he would hold a beer glass.

"This morning," she announced, "I fully intend to start."

At the very thought, Roger Antill, who'd barely glanced in her direction, blew out his cheeks.

"I'm very much looking forward to going through your brother's papers," she said.

For a while he remained nodding. Then he closed his eyes. "I've got a better idea."

He'd give her a conducted tour over the place, the bulging paddocks, the eucalypts at mid-distance, the dams, the old yards, the flocks of sheep—the works. They'd bounce around in his dented ute, the two dogs keeping balance on the back.

"Should we wait for Sophie?"

"Let's go." Already he had his hat on. "I'm not going to bite you."

15

THERE WERE men past sixty who had seen a lot—their interestingly mangled appearances. Some had been through hell in Europe or up in the islands, and God knows how many marriage breakups. Others had endured economic hardship, rural and urban. Did experience of strange and difficult countries make a difference? Some had fled for their lives. Men otherwise living quietly had lost wives, children, brothers before their own parents. Surely they'd have news.

Being a witness to death, or almost death, or to suffering—at least to be in the vicinity of extremes—would perhaps reveal the occasional truth not available in ordinary life.

These were Wesley's thoughts, obscurely felt, back then.

At St. Vincent's Hospital he got a job as a porter. It was not hard work. The doctors and nurses took their rapid strides. Brown lino shining. His job was to deliver crutches, and wheel patients along corridors and into cavernous lifts to be x-rayed or operated on. In these circumstances, women were willing and easier to talk to than the horizontal men, who all looked as if they were severely wounded in battle and reaching out for the cigarette.

Between shifts the porters sat outside on the concrete, white coats undone, and smoked and drank tea, and stared down at their shoes. In broad daylight they were a pale, blotchy, weary-looking bunch. One of them might announce the price of a haircut had gone up. No reply, just the faint sound of cigarettes being dragged on. Opinions on politicians and football results were delivered without pity, without expecting a reply. A heavy unsmiling man did most of the talking. His name sounded like Sheldrake. Early on, he turned to Wesley, sitting on one side. "What have you got to say for yourself?" A heavy presence, bald, except for a ring of yellowish hair, the way corn soup has overflowed a saucepan—as if his head could keep only a certain amount of information. He introduced topics. That very morning he was pushing into a lift and a wheel fell off his trolley, almost tipping out an old woman, which hardly rated a nod, since it had happened at one time to each of them. Did you know there was not one but two conspiracies to shoot President Kennedy? In the navy they've now got women going down in submarines. Have you ever heard anything so fucking ludicrous? When it came to the nurses, the Irish ones, and from there to women in general, the tone was detailed, vehement and dismissive, the idea being to gain wry agreement.

Seated on his bar stool like a tennis umpire, this man Sheldrake waited for them to bat a conversation back and forth. The strong suggestion was they were not fulfilling their potential. As he stared at one, then another, they in turn leaned back on their assorted cane, tubular steel or perforated plastic chairs, and if one of them did say something it was usually an entirely fresh topic.

Wesley's chair was a wooden one. It had an uncomfortable dark-stained ordinariness, a nineteen-fifties kitchen chair, and with it the memories of a certain Australian childhood, which didn't concern Wesley but apparently put off some of the others. The day he arrived it had been the only one left, and he sat on it; he grew accustomed to the cobwebbed concrete and putting his feet up, always taking a position against the wall near a dripping tap. It was a lapse, a space. Traffic along Barcom Avenue, and farther away Oxford Street, rose and fell in a blurry regularity, as waves come forward and dissolve on a beach. And voices, faint.

It was while half-listening to the others there in the sun that Wesley decided to begin thinking in a less pedantic manner. And he should begin now before it was too late. He thought of his father and his stamps. By following Clive Renmark's recommendation and first concentrating on the Greeks, he had moved on in regular stages to the Moderns, soaking up everything he could lay his hands on. The discoveries of each philosopher allowed each subsequent philosopher to climb up onto their shoulders, as if philosophy was a form of gymnastics, from where they could climb still higher, or at any rate lean out at an angle while still holding on. All his available time spent scaling the tremendous peaks of Western thought had left Wesley with the uncomfortable feeling his own mind was dutiful, pedantic, unoriginal. Clearly it was because his studies had followed a chronological path. In his apartment the books and journals piled on shelves, on the floor, on his unmade bed pointed to a free-ranging, seriously unconventional mind at work. This was the harbor city where cars rust and pages of books fox. Wesley had taken to underlining and scribbling comments in the margins, and made "copious," as Rosie next door liked to joke, notes. Already he had formed the habit of writing statements on scraps of paper and sticking them on walls and mirrors, so he could reconsider them.

Rosie Steig was impressed with his industry. Now and then Wesley would pause and rub his eyes in wonder. Other times he'd say, aloud, "I *don't* think so." ("All swans are white." Not where I come from!) It was enough for Rosie to lift her head. They were friends. If a book he required was out of print, and if he couldn't pick up an old copy at one of the shops in Glebe, she happily borrowed for him at the Fisher Library.

Wesley was finding a gap existed between the clarity of his chosen subject and the softer, unavoidable intrusions of everyday life.

Rosie Steig often came in and lay on the sofa and studied one of her many subjects, while he sat at his desk studying one subject, his cheeks pressed between his palms, like a stone face on the corner of an old building. Not even her ostentatious yawns broke his concentration.

From the sofa and hidden from him, Rosie called out, "What is her name? Mrs. Something—what do you see in her?"

Virginia Kentridge was old enough to be his mother.

"I'll tell you tomorrow. Maybe next week."

"I want to know now."

"What is it you want to know exactly?"

Virginia Kentridge had none of Rosie's casual generosity; hers was anxious. There was a restlessness in Virginia Kentridge, her impatient widow's body, and the way she thought and spoke, different from his mother, or his sister even, more of a series of blinks—becoming for him a complicating factor. Sometimes he noticed when she spoke she appeared not to be talking to him at all.

Standing before him, she pointed out how her skin was smooth, look, stomach nicely flattish, and—"Don't you like them?" Because of his studies he had become solemn, silent, single-minded. He was always somewhere else. As a consequence, she didn't want him working in the hospital, especially since he didn't need to work at all. "Have you washed your hands? I don't want you coming near me, if you haven't."

In the bathroom one night, Wesley found Virginia weeping. She had noticed the first gray pubic hair; no amount of reasonable words comforted her. When he later told Rosie she looked up and said, "Poor Virginia."

Working in the hospital he could think about the philosophical problems he had encountered that very morning. But the wards and the corridors, the chirpy, red-nosed nurses, and the patients in their helplessness, represented the close-by world, only more so. It wasn't only the regular sight of stoicism.

On a Thursday he arrived as usual with his mug of tea at the concrete courtyard to see the heavy talkative one had taken his chair—not just sitting on it, sitting in that fat-arsed, over-casual way. Antill went across and while the man was talking pulled the chair out from under him. In the struggle Sheldrake fell onto the concrete and getting up was about to spring at Antill.

"Whoa! Take it easy!"—they were holding him back, as if he was a horse. "Here we are, slaving our guts out to save lives, and you two are trying to kill each other."

It was a fight over a wooden chair, which Antill would later use to describe his struggle for a new philosophy.

16

ERICA, WHO was holding on to the door—just his thumb and forefinger keeping them on track—hand closest often changing down to first—saw how his way of conversing, which had plenty more stops and starts and false trails than actual words, followed the contours of the meandering landscape. Having to negotiate the unevenness on a daily basis had infected his speech. And when coming out with a sentence of more than three words he closed his eyes, the eyelids fluttering slightly as he spoke. The last person she had seen with this visual stammer (if that is what it is) was a Methodist minister with ginger eyelashes who visited her mother in Adelaide, and so remained fixed in her memory seated in the lounge room with cup of tea balanced on a floral saucer in one hand, while taking a bite out of a piece of sponge cake.

As for Roger Antill, he just then wasn't about to look across at this woman from Sydney. After getting her out of the house he began to ask himself if it had been a good idea. For one thing, he wondered whether she wanted to see land and more land, and hear about the never-ending tasks of a grazier. City people had their own interests, own areas of expertise. He didn't want to bore or confuse her, even though boring another person could sometimes become interesting.

Roger Antill stopped. Looking down over the steering wheel he indicated with his chin the original property. Chimney the only thing left of a hut, ironbark posts as gray as newsprint, lines of fence wire here and there—signs barely decipherable, as if underwater.

These were the traces left by his ancestors. Roger A. mentioned some of their solid English names, and how they died—headfirst over horses, diphtheria, as cannon fodder in Belgium and France. Daughters who went to Sydney, then on to London, came back only for visits, if at all.

Turning off the track, the homestead well behind them, he swerved over the bare ground which fell away to the left, where there was an overflowing creek, rattling and frothing, clotted with wet-black sticks, leaves, branches of trees. At one point he banged into a waterlogged burrow and swore. "Now what do you make of that?" Still steering with one hand, "By myself I wouldn't have said anything, not a word."

How nature erases the previous day. After rain it returns changed, but basically the same.

Sheep stood about in the paddocks on either side. Many lambs, pale.

It was a curvaceous part of the earth, displaying the most natural declivities, casual harmony over gradual distances. Erica allowed herself to blend into gullies, where the same land allowed itself to rise into a nicotine-stained hill spotted with white-trunked trees.

"Amazing what you see when you look at something long enough. We have hills here that look like a woman's bum, and whatnot. That gully over there. What does it look like?" For some reason Erica felt respected, and she smiled. "The knees, elbows. I pointed to these . . . eye associations . . . pointed them out to my brother, Wesley, not long after he came back. He said to me, 'Yes, all right. The trouble is you're not the first in the world to notice this. It follows that as an idea it becomes reduced to the ordinary.'"

To lighten the conversation, Roger put on a stifled yawn.

"After that," he said in an extra loud voice, "I thought it best to leave the fancy thinking to him."

Erica was laughing.

"I decided to stick to what I know—whatever that is. Opening gates! I can do that."

He got out, opened it, drove through, closed it and got going again. At the next, Erica leapt out—"I'm going to do this"—to give him a hand.

The irritating gate, it was being difficult. As she struggled she imagined his eyes wandering over her waist and hips. He had nowhere else to look. Joining her at the gate he was patient and jokey as he demonstrated the slight twist to ease the chain and washer over the bolt.

"I never got to ask Wesley how it was philosophy got the better of him. There's no other sign of it in the family."

It was as if philosophy was a disease. Erica asked if his brother had worked on his papers all day.

For a while the remaining brother said nothing. It looked as if he had gone back to hardly-talking.

"I suppose you could say Prodigal Son. There were aspects of that. I was . . . fifteen when our brother shot off to Sydney. I didn't see much of him after that. We'd get postcards, snow on mountains, little houses, that sort of thing. He was in Europe, you know. With the death of our father, he telegrammed to say it was time to come back. Fair enough." As if his memory was attached to a well-oiled spring, his eyelids began fluttering. "The day he stepped off the train . . . I walked straight past him. I couldn't fit a face to him. It also had something to do with the hair. It had turned white."

Stopping and starting—fading too—these sentences drew Erica into listening carefully, which she did while noticing the many new shapes, objects and compositions appearing mid-distant and far, on all sides. There were long puddles and stretches of mud.

Here Erica pointed across the driver to a bend in the same overflowing creek, to where a ewe was stuck, just its head showing.

Before Roger stopped she was out onto the muddy ground. She rolled up her trousers, and waded out to the animal. The cold rush of water made her feel determined. It was a demonstration. All around her was brown swirling.

"She'll weigh a ton," he called out. "Leave her for me."

Taking one more step—an animal was life—its bulging eyes—the weight of water shifted her foot off a slippery rock. She fell forward onto the net of wet branches trapping the ewe, and the animal sank under her weight. As Roger took her by the arm and pulled her out she saw the sheep floating away, rolling in the current.

"I was all right. But thank you."

Erica remained staring at the sheep.

"It wasn't deep. And I'm not entirely helpless." Also she could swim. She seemed to be talking to herself. "What are you laughing at? It looked as if an animal was in the midst of drowning."

Now she'd lost sight of the sheep. And she wanted above all to keep seeing it. As long as it didn't die under the immense, almost white sky. To one side, he was gazing in the opposite direction at one of the paddocks.

Suddenly she could have shoved or punched him.

"You don't care. Out here you become accustomed to the suffering of animals. It happens all around you—every single day. It's part of the general situation. There might be an animal in pain, but you just get on with the job, don't you? What does it matter to you? Each animal is merely a unit—I don't want to say a cog—in the vast machine which is the producing farm."

"You sound like Wesley. Different voice, that's all. All up here." He tapped his forehead.

In wet trousers and top Erica climbed into the ute, folded her arms. Once more a misunderstanding. And it had happened early. Breathing through her mouth, she asked herself why it typically had to be like this. A mismatch of opinion or the way of expressing it triggered in her a sharper observation of a person's defects, which suddenly protruded the way rocks appear in a paddock. It was awkward now sitting next to him. She felt unsettled. What was that all about? If she brought her intellect into the situation she knew he would suffer; and so she hadn't. Sooner or later every man presented difficulties; and those difficulties came forward and remained almost as physical shapes. The other person as obstacle! It was why she allowed herself to live alone. She felt unadorned.

Just the one hand resting on the wheel, Roger Antill appeared unconcerned. He didn't have a clue what was going through her head. The men she came across were formidable for all the wrong reasons. An exception was Sophie's father, the manufacturer. She was pleasantly hypnotized by the size of his head, and with it his experienced, deep-voweled rotund way of talking. Her life was more placid in Sydney. She was holding on to the door again as they slowly drove downstream to where the creek widened. Seated beside her this man consisted of a large number of gaps. Everything he did or said was unsatisfactory to Erica, even when they saw ahead a sodden sheep struggle out of the shallows, and he said nothing.

By the time they returned to the homestead her clothes had dried.

From the veranda Sophie stood up from the planter's chair and came forward.

"Where have you been? Why didn't you let me know? You know I would want to go. I don't understand you."

As Roger sauntered off, Sophie's confusion overflowed into Erica.

"Why did you do this?"

"I don't want to talk about it."

Following her into the house, Sophie whispered, "What's happened here?"

Now it was Sophie's turn to examine her friend's confusion and be saddened by it; or so it seemed.

"Please stop it. We've been looking over the property,

that's all, the extent of it, the scenery. We saw sheep and trees."

"Yes. And?"

Erica couldn't explain it either.

"The creek's turned into a torrent. Apparently it was a fox in the distance, running at an angle. Overall it was interesting."

"You're not saying anything. Try me again."

To get a result, Sophie occasionally used a small amount of dynamite.

For when Erica spoke it was as if she wasn't interested in herself. She barely said "I." Instead, Erica's absorption in thought as a subject made her appear impersonal—which in turn was beginning to concern her. Already she was having doubts about her reaction to Roger Antill. She didn't know what had got into her. If it had registered with him at all he'd see she was a stony, opinionated woman who flew off the handle—and she wasn't like that, not really.

The smaller woolshed of unpainted corrugated iron, patched with lighter gray sheets, had a slight tilt and two blank windows (no curtains). A woman could never fail to be amazed at how close it was to the house. Imagine: during shearing and crutching all those sheep crowding the yards, as more and more arrived, the dogs running around in semicircles, and the rich collective smell of sheep, the clouds of dust kicked up, and the extra flies—not to mention the constant foul language of men knee-deep in sheep that the women in the house could not block from their ears. For this reason, and as the property grew in size and the flocks multiplied, the shed in the mid nineteen-thirties was replaced by a much larger one, positioned at a good distance from the house.

Machinery and buildings no longer used on sheep stations are left where they are. Over the seasons they change color and subside, attracting rust, weeds and patient shadow, as they return to the earth, though not entirely.

On the afternoon Wesley returned in his lightweight suit, and after washing his face and hands he went over to the small woolshed with Roger and Lindsey in tow, and pulled open the door. They stepped inside. Lines of silver light from the loose-fitting sheets of corrugated iron, and the various nail holes piercing the walls, intersected the brown stillness, silent from its previous activity, and illuminated the wool table like an altar. Along one side the wooden pens were in shadow.

"Almost, but not quite cathedral," Wesley reportedly said, which had Roger and Lindsey scratching their heads. Evidently, Wesley still had one foot back in the old world. If it was all right by them, he'd like to take over the shed as his place of work.

17

FOLLOWING HIS struggle with Wesley Antill the orderly known as Sheldrake didn't appear again in the courtyard. His stool stood empty. Surrounded by the different chairs occupied by figures each producing smoke, the chrome legs supporting a red vinyl seat took on a stubborn, accusatory presence. To Wesley the slit in the cheap red seat seemed to be pointing the finger directly at him. After all, it was he who . . . The other orderlies appeared unconcerned, but since the little scuffle to regain his chair he felt they had accepted him less easily, even though he hadn't before taken much notice of them.

Without Sheldrake there to crack the whip the conversation was certainly desultory.

Then one of them sat down and came out with his name.

"Poor old Hendrik, I hear he's got cancer."

"Who told you that?"

"Cancer where?" Wesley asked.

Hendrik—has a Dutch ring; an English father, by the look.

Someone made a sympathetic clicking sound.

"You can't possibly think it's your fault," Mrs. Kentridge cried out, as soon as he mentioned it.

And when Wesley had told Rosie about the chair incident and the altered mood of the others she stopped what she was doing—writing a long letter to her married sister—and to his surprise concentrated on the problem (what "problem"?), and asked detailed questions from every conceivable angle, the original cubist, trying to give a shape to the situation. Analyzing possible reasons-for could absorb Rosie for hours at a time.

"Anyway, he's in strife now."

"I can see you having a shocking temper," she said, still thinking of the business with the chair. And not for the first time she asked, "Why is that?"

"The emotions are a difficult category," was all he could say—attempt at a joke. "I am working on it."

Strange how lead-footed he became during these conversations, even with Rosie. Wesley had wanted his chair back; it was his. That was all. But to march up and simply lunge at Sheldrake—where was David Hume's courtesy of argument? He wondered whether the plainness of the dry-grass rural life could be responsible.

Every day he and Rosie spoke to each other, and the nights he wasn't at Virginia Kentridge's they slept together. More and more Wesley wanted to talk to somebody about his latest philosophical understanding or misunderstandings, really a thinking aloud. It was sometimes a matter of shaking off a loose idea. While he tried to narrow his way of seeing, Rosie encouraged him here and there to enrich his way of seeing. She had a broad take on subjects parallel to philosophy—religious thought and three ancient languages being some—which filled out her voice and shadowy flesh, her lips, and scented her skin, at least as far as Wesley was concerned. Areas of soaked-up learning had added to her; they were hidden, but came out as generosity. Her mouth was open. "I don't want to be regarded as something like a sister," she said late one night. By then they were sleeping naked, his wrist warming her waist.

Wesley asked if he could bring Rosie to one of his mother's Thursday soirees. To be on the safe side, Mrs. Antill didn't invite any of her friends. From the sofa she held out her hand and let it droop. "Excuse this," she apologized, "I am feeling fragile these days." Mrs. Antill wore a wheat-colored satin dressing gown which added to her leisured watchfulness. She had a steady handsome face containing trace elements of Wesley's jaw, all the more interesting for being haggard. Although she looked carefully at the younger woman she wasn't sure what to make of her.

Walking home Rosie said, "Definitely a statement, your mother stretched out there on the couch."

"I haven't seen her like that before," Wesley admitted.

"She's smaller than I thought. I liked her. Is she still not speaking to your friend, the black widow?"

Virginia Kentridge? In the space of an evening she'd go through three or four different moods. Overall she insisted on pulling him towards her; wanting to keep him there. Virginia was serious about this. During the day she couldn't understand why he couldn't be there, and when he was there how his mind seemed to be somewhere else. His large presence in her house, inside her, it was almost enough; for they didn't talk much. She dressed up for him. She could be shameless. There was a general moist breathlessness, as when she directed his head to between her legs, as if there was not a lot of time.

For Wesley it became confusing. It was not something he could discuss with Rosie, and as a sign of loss of interest he was especially attentive to Virginia—and in turn her happy response confused him further.

With some difficulty he found where Sheldrake lived. It was near the hospital, off Forbes Street, a ground floor one-bedroom in a brown building without a locked entrance; Hendrik kept his front door ajar, to entice people to enter.

When Wesley knocked and poked his head in, he showed no surprise.

"This is mighty kind of you. The rest of those bastards couldn't give a shit."

"They said to say hello."

"No-hopers all of them."

In flannel pajamas on special from Woolworth's, Sheldrake lay in bed, just a sheet covering the immense rise of his stomach which heated the entire room.

"It's all here," he prodded, "running amok as I speak. It's in the stomach area. The bowel, liver, lungs. Nothing can be done. I had been feeling a bit tired, that's all."

Wesley realized that at the hospital Sheldrake's usual elongated stool would have been uncomfortable.

Tomorrow, Sheldrake was due in the hospice. "Take a seat!"

And Wesley too gave a smile at their recent history.

Everybody was trying to be funny, while he wanted to remain serious. Why he had made the visit he wasn't at all sure. He looked around the room. In the corner was a neat selection of news magazines. A bookshelf had on display a concise Oxford and an encyclopedia held together by a ginger rubber band. Above, in a gilt frame, was a photo-realist scene of a perfectly mirrored lake surrounded by snow and pine trees.

"Tell me something I don't know."

Wesley had always liked this aspect of Sheldrake, the large man, now having trouble breathing. Wasn't it Schopenhauer who placed a gold coin on his café table every day, as he ate his lunch, to encourage one of the gawping onlookers to say something—anything—that would be of interest to him? (And any takers? Not one.)

"Can I make you a cup of tea, or anything?"

Sheldrake shook his head and looked up at the ceiling.

"How's the pain?"

"I already know that."

"Pain, I haven't had much experience of." Virginia would have quickly said, "Touch wood!"

"You have something to look forward to."

Wesley wanted to know if he was afraid. What can it all possibly amount to—being alive, on two feet, and being aware of it, then, after a short time, it coming to an end.

Instead, he stood up to examine the walls which he noticed had been papered over with printed pages, the walls blurring with columns of words, sentences.

"That's the Holy Scriptures you're looking at," Sheldrake turned his head. "If you're interested."

He had never thought of Sheldrake being religious.

"I've glued them on the wall, as an *aide memoire*. Do you know what an *aide memoire* is?"

Wesley said nothing.

"I don't know what's worse, the Old Testament or the New," Sheldrake said in a loud voice. "I've glued them up in case I forget what a load of baloney it all is. I want to be reminded every day. Pick a verse there, any verse and read it out. Do you see what I'm getting at?"

Now his ring of yellow hair took on the fallen halo look as he became stuck in a convulsion of hacking, spitting and reddening.

"I'm being punished." He tried laughing, only to cough still further.

"I was about to say," Wesley remained standing, "the accumulation of facts doesn't always add up to much."

Did this man alone under the sheet have a wife somewhere? A few children discarded along the way? What about a black-sheep brother trying to grow coffee in New Guinea? A younger sister out at Bankstown bringing up three kids after the father shot through?

"You're a thoughtful character, I see that," Sheldrake searched around with his words. "You're probably smarter than me. I didn't mind the hospital. The job was a good one . . . the sitting around and talking out in the sun. I liked it."

Wesley waited as the large man closed his eyes.

"Thank you, thank you. I'll give it a rest now."

Hendrik Sheldrake would remain a small unraveled knot in Antill's life—unexplained.

The day, shortly afterwards, he died in the hospice was the day Wesley found his mother on the floor by the sofa, the television on. After phoning his father, Wesley sat by the window with its view of the Botanic Gardens, and ransacked the philosophers to explain turmoil, better still to correct it—his first life-shock. Only later would answers be available. Instead of being comforted by Rosie, it was Wesley who held her, as if he was comforting her, and for the first time slipped in, necessarily hectic in their immediate life-producing movements; once, and once more.

Rosie stroked his nose with her little finger.

"What might you be thinking?"

"I'm not sure yet."

He was thinking it was time he hardened himself. Part of the attraction of softness was the enveloping sense of blurriness, while he wanted as much as possible to preserve the outline of his own self. As a result, he thought his understanding of the most serious of all subjects, philosophy, had become more and more out of reach. It was a mishmash of the thoughts of others. Local complications, responses, confusions were coming in from all directions. It was true that a close-by death introduced a form of hardness. The death of a parent was nothing less than a before/after moment. He was an altered person. Already he looked at the world differently. And it was a long time since he had been forced into attempting to think clearly about what lay not on the page, but directly in life in front of him.

Wesley hadn't been returning Virginia's calls. It was she who had been holding her lean finger on the buzzer to his door. If she'd had a rock she'd have thrown it through the window.

She posted a card. "Is this a serious person, or what?"

She was right. But in some areas he couldn't do much better. He wrote, "I'm sorry." Quickly added, "It's time I left."

Later, with Rosie, he could hear himself sounding furtive. His words were not accurate enough. And yet in trying to be true to himself he considered he had the best of intentions—even though he wasn't sure where he was going. Several times he said very firmly, carefully, he would keep in touch.

18

THE GREATEST of the great philosophers followed the solitary life, a life of relative simplicity, living alone, in that sense a hard life, just the candle on the table, whereas the founder of psychoanalysis and his disciples and rivals enjoyed married lives, children and gardens which provided the warmth and intimacy of the softer life. The philosopher is interested in silence. The psychoanalyst is drawn to the other person, to words strung out; they're prepared to encourage the horizontal halting sentences, faint noise of traffic outside, someone on the street shouting. Spare a thought for these conduits in comfortable clothing: after listening at regular set intervals to a procession of people one by one thinking aloud about themselves, they return home in the evening to encounter more words, more cries for attention, where they are expected to apply not ordinary everyday understanding, but unusual additional understanding.

More and more Sydney has come to resemble a word-factory the way it produces extra, spoken words.

Psychoanalysts have not seen the need to set up rooms away from the city (Sydney). An overlay of voices and other distractions has separated city dwellers from their natural selves, in turn aggravating all manner of obstructions, confusions, the specifically named phobias, which cry out for treatment. It is the philosophers who have shown a penchant for pastoral areas, often up in the mountains. There's been quite a history of it; many distinguished names hiding themselves away. And then what happened? The remoteness of the places the philosophers chose as their "work worlds" drew curiosity and respect from the city dwellers who couldn't help embroidering the distant uncomfortable huts, towers, the forests and lakes, until they became further isolated and frozen in the aura of myth.

The "comings and goings" of the seasons, the firm statement of geology, above all the absence of voices, can provide a feeling of closeness to the original nature of things, the beginning from where an explanation can begin to be constructed. There—in the mountains especially—philosophy can be seen as a natural force.

19

ON THE third or fourth day, Erica entered the small woolshed.

Already the day was warm.

Never having stepped inside such a shed before she remained near the door, not sure what to take in first.

The air was thick with the smell of wool, so thick it surrounded and began caressing her. Erica felt if she stayed here for any length of time her skin would improve. A few handfuls of wool had been left on the floor. Light came in through holes in the tin walls, as if the place had been shot up, and ragged gaps here and there let in more, and so the irregular patterns of silver on the floor and opposite walls. Otherwise the space was mostly shadow.

It took a moment to adjust to the light.

A wheat bag had been nailed up over the nearest window. Down the far end the other window illuminated a corner, which had a table, a chair and shelves holding stacks of paper. On the table were pages of manuscript and the white of these pages gleamed in patches and brightened the corner almost electrically. Other sheets of paper seemed to flutter white in midair.

Erica took a step forward. Then she strode over to Wesley Antill's work table. Beneath the window was a horsehair sofa and blanket; through the window, the ground sloped up towards a hill.

She sat in Antill's chair. Within reach was a tray of fresh quarto, and next to it pages filled with writing, some in pencil, and a notebook. The black fountain pen, made in Germany; there would have to be an ink bottle somewhere. There was not much else: a pencil sharpener bolted to the table, a saucer containing paper clips and rubber bands, and a small traveler's clock (Roman numerals) in a leather case. Also on the table was a bottle of tomato sauce, almost finished, the leftovers clinging to the insides, like the remnants of the British Empire on a map. The sauce bottle certainly added to the atmosphere of almost brutal plainness, so much so that Erica couldn't help imagining the philosopher in his underpants, gaunt, arms tanned up to his elbows, always with an appetite. And she wondered again if, in order to think deeply, it was necessary to live and work in barren surroundings.

She got up and moved around the table and touched the pages in loose piles on the shelves. These too were filled with his handwriting. Still more were stacked on the floor; no doubt false starts, or faulty ideas, or ideas veering off the chosen path. There must have been many hundreds of pages. Erica noticed she was standing on discarded pages lying on the floor. She went back to the chair again. Strange to be sitting where he sat. She had her elbows on the table. The pages in front of her would be the ones Antill was working on when he died, the Prodigal Son. But she could hardly even glance at them. Before beginning anything she'd have to find the beginning in amongst the papers.

She leaned back and looked around. The woolshed had the extra stillness of a place where work and well-oiled equipment had been abandoned. Only then did she look closely at the pages pegged onto a length of string, like white handkerchiefs hanging out to dry.

Antill had written, in his blue ink, statements to spur him on. At his work table, he had only to turn his head slightly to see them.

Begin with nothing, begin again.

Next, *Not to think, but allow thinking to arrive.* These pages were fastened by plastic pegs of various colors, *Drought-thoughts.*

A smaller piece torn from his notebook had turned yellow, *With no hesitation, none. Otherwise—.*

On the nearest sheet of suspended paper in extra-large writing was a line she recognized. Evidently for Wesley Antill it summed up the philosopher's task: philosophy was *a confession on the part of its author, a kind of involuntary and unconscious memoir.*

It was the quote Professor Thursk in the lecture hall or in the quadrangle was fond of dismissing with a good-natured chuckle ("that old chestnut"), as he did with anything

German, or almost-German—which had been enough for Erica to think there was perhaps something to it. And now here it was on a piece of paper hanging in a woolshed.

In considering a philosophy, she would be considering a life.

Erica didn't hear Roger Antill arrive.

"Have you made any sense of it yet?"

"Do you mind? I'm thinking."

Erica flinched at the sound of her sharpness. She was turning into a severe woman, a sharp, methodical, increasingly assertive type—and who could be bothered with them? It went with her face which she considered too small. She wondered why she had developed a hard side—how unnecessary it was. Roger Antill was not a bad man; and he owned the woolshed.

As if nothing had happened, he went over to the bookshelves.

"He had a brain, all right. Our brother was brainy. He had the means of concentration. Nothing would stand in the way. I've seen similar in fine-wool breeders, successful, and the old Hungarian who runs the post office in town— he takes photographs of every bird that lands on his back fence. Single-minded. Except Wes had the extra brains, no doubt about it. Can a person use their brain too much? He never gave his brain a rest. My sister asked me to see if you need anything. There's a teapot over there."

Before she could answer, he moved across to the window, his back to her and, by not talking, silenced her.

After the way she had spoken, Erica wasn't sure what to say anyway. She couldn't stop thinking about herself.

"There used to be eucalypts out here, a nice lot of red gums. He didn't want to see them when he worked, he told us. He went out and attacked them with a chainsaw. I gave him a hand.

"It wasn't that he had anything against eucalypts, although they were measly with shade, it was that he wanted no distractions. They reminded him too much of where he was."

For a good five minutes neither spoke.

"Wes sure was unlike anyone I had come across."

He turned from the window.

"If you're not careful, you could end up sitting here for the next twenty years trying to work him out. How would that be?"

A casual, entrenched skepticism had straightened his mouth, not unpleasantly. And out of local habit he bent down and picked up a bit of old wool and measured it between his fingers.

"Can you take this away, please?"—pointing to the bottle of tomato sauce. "It makes me unhappy looking at it."

As always he was in his dusty working trousers and boots; and before she could say anything more he had gone.

The hours passed quietly in the perforated darkness. Of course the philosopher's chair had to be a hard wooden one. Now and then she went over to the window and contemplated the treeless scene; fresh shoots had erupted from the stumps and in the spaces in between. Around lunchtime Erica stepped out and stood near the veranda. She stretched her arms over her head and squinted into the mid-distance and beyond. Aloud she said, "Sweep of landscape." As she took in the breadth of it, Erica, from inner-Sydney—a city of verticals—some ragged undulations—blue glitter—tried to see why she felt an affinity to the landscape: "gradualness" was what she decided. The slow rise and roundness. Gradual were the patterns, no limestone outcrops, gorges, river, no patch of green grass; no sharp lines of black, either. Gradualness possessed an endlessness.

This old dry part of the earth laid out before her was familiar, which seemed to reduce Erica's apprehension of the pages, enough for her to experience a flow of contentment which reached back to the familiarity of a few people and places in Sydney.

"Look at you," said Sophie in the kitchen.

Seated also at the table, Lindsey gave her the welcome smile which lengthened her face—the shoebox tilting.

"I've decided something," Erica announced, because she was restless. "I'm too analytical. I've now realized this."

"That's my department," Sophie gave a single clap. "That's exactly what I'm like! I find I'm always making a basic situation more complex than it needs to be. All sorts of side issues come into the equation, which happens to be simple enough and staring me in the face. It causes no end of difficulty." The happily married lecturer, of the English woolen socks, being a recent example.

Erica noticed the tomato sauce bottle on the table. Even there in the kitchen it appeared to be standing for the plain and bleak life, of hunger satisfied, wipe the plate with thumb or crust; her hand involuntarily made to shove it back into the cupboard, out of view.

"I intervene in my mind—and too early," Erica insisted. "I can't seem to help it. In reducing the argument, I reduce the person. I can hear myself becoming sharp." The last thing she wanted was for it to become permanent. "I think your brother," she glanced at Lindsey, "has found me so."

"Is that why we're like this, sitting here, all three of us?" Sophie laughed. She had spoken scarcely six words to what's-his-name, the brother. Where was he now?

Lindsey had remained looking at Erica, "Roger? He wouldn't notice. In this area he's as blind as a bat. Hopeless."

The way sisters dismiss (affectionately) their poor brothers, and vice versa.

"I'm going to improve," Erica said, more to herself. Again she checked if she had sounded severe, speaking through the gritted teeth, et cetera.

Sophie inquired about the philosopher's papers.

"It's going to take more than a few hours." More like weeks, Erica thought, and wasn't displeased.

Sophie frowned. "Haven't you actually looked at them yet? I'm going to have to get back soon."

"We've only just arrived, have we not?"

At this point a phone rang which had Sophie rushing to her large handbag and swearing as she tried to find it.

"Hello, Daddy? Are you all right?"

She went out onto the veranda to talk. It allowed Erica to turn to Lindsey with careful questions about her brothers, hoping to anticipate the soon to be seen "unconscious memoir" of the philosopher, if that's what it was. The smallest bits of information added, or gave flesh, to the picture. Apparently for lunch Wesley ate a boiled egg and a piece of ham, and had green tea in small packets posted on the first of each month from Chinatown in Sydney. He sipped his tea from a small cup; anyone would think he'd been to China. Erica then asked about Roger. As they chatted she noticed Sophie glancing at her through the window.

With a puzzled face, Sophie came in and handed Erica her phone. "He doesn't want to talk to me. He wants to talk to you."

20

EACH AND every perhaps and possibly, on the one hand this, on the other hand that, yes but, along with the ifs, the maybes, the not necessarilies, while producing an appearance of tolerance and abstraction, which made him attractive in the eyes of others, had spread and undermined the haphazard foundations of Wesley Antill's own opinions. Hang on, let me think. (He began talking to himself.) Lack of precision—that is, how to be yourself, *as much as possible*—tightened its grip; uncertainty was OK, confusion not.

The complications of everyday life added to the confusion, as if Mrs. Kentridge in black and the softer but no less demanding intimacy of Rosie Steig had been placed close by in order to occupy and actually deflect his thoughts.

And when Wesley Antill began his wanderings, carrying his mother's suitcase, and for the first time in his life set foot on foreign soil, he chose as his destination a city not known as a center for philosophy; in fact, it had hardly made a contribution at all. Antill could have headed straight for Edinburgh, or Amsterdam, Copenhagen, Paris even, as well as any number of German cities and villages, let alone Athens.

He chose London, not intending to stay long.

In the train from Heathrow, Antill looked at the bright green parks and into the backyards of narrow houses, the traffic slowly moving along the streets—little cars, vans—and people waiting on platforms before entering the carriage on their way to work. Slate and brownish houses folded in behind him. He could get away with murder here. The farther he went in, not knowing a soul, the more anonymous he felt.

The first hotel was almost next door to the British Library. After a restless night he stepped out and noticed he had been trying to sleep in the shadow of hundreds of tons of paper, millions, more like trillions, of printed, never-resting words. Those desperate descriptions, classifications, explanations and rhyming couplets under the one roof. It was not what he wanted just then. Another hotel in W2 he left after experiencing their nylon sheets. Smell of gas in another. These were small discomforts. And he was not one to complain. Wesley marveled at the utilitarian breakfasts, the fried eggs turned with rare skill, an obvious specialty of the British. He moved from one hotel to the next. It was a way of mastering the enormous mass of the city. He took rooms in boardinghouses, Kensington, Golder's Green, Putney, Clapham, Kensal Rise—and moved on. A succession of landlords—lord, what an exaggeration—and your typical vigilant landlady of the crinkled throat and powdered nose. To them, his worldly possessions appeared to be contained in a medium-size suitcase, its fine leather (Simpson's of Piccadilly?) spotted by the landladies, and so without being aware of it Antill received extra-attentive service.

He wrote to Lindsey, not to trot out the usual about Eng/London, but knowing his sister, sitting and writing and waiting in the backblocks of New South Wales, was interested in rainfall, wherever it was.

"Early days, I know, but it hasn't so much as drizzled yet. I'm looking forward to the cold, and I wouldn't say it's been cold yet." He didn't tell her it was bloody freezing.

Sitting in a bus or on a bench outdoors he couldn't help thinking of Rosie—it was at random, the voice, and the way she positioned herself in the world, the warmth of her body. By leaving Sydney in a rush he had abused her devotion, and he considered getting her to join him. But before long he returned to being firm and went on moving about in this impervious grubby immensity, alone.

It would soon exhaust itself. He was under the flight path. He was too close to the railway line. Through the walls a bus driver berated his passengers in his sleep. Radio and television coming through. The cobbled courtyard in Blackfriars must have once been stables. The baby was crying. Too many married couples next door having their yelling matches. Basement of the Nash terrace house. The mews a stone's throw from Westminster. Somebody being sick. He wondered where he fitted in. Was that not important? Terrible rising damp. What about the stand-up comedian through the wall in Cleveland Square rehearsing his lines—clearing his throat and beginning again? The mildest people wanted to make friends. And it was hard to avoid the music. The different streets, the many different pale and lumpy faces. More than a year had passed. Moving from one place to the next allowed him to avoid thinking, at least in any sustained, directed way; at the same time he believed he was experiencing the apparent complexity of the place. He was "finding his feet by walking," he informed his sister.

Wesley finally settled for a third-floor flat in a crescent just before Shepherd's Bush. The house next door had each floor taken up by a painter with an international reputation, whose canvases consisted of stripes, mostly horizontal, of various colors. Much depended on a steady hand. Accordingly, each room on each floor of the painter's house had fluorescent lighting, the only one in the crescent like it, a sort of lighthouse always glowing at one end.

He went wandering at night too, as he did in Sydney—the philosopher of the streets.

He bought water-resistant tan shoes, and an expensive, spring-loaded umbrella.

On Holland Park Avenue, opposite the Russian Consulate, Wesley reached out to pat a dalmatian, and was bitten by it. A short wide woman in a black tracksuit came forward, very confident. Shaped like a cello, and taking small steps, she had querulous eyes. Wesley also saw her black hair, which fell like a horse's tail down to the small of her back, where Wesley, coming off the farm, expected it abruptly to swish, as it would at an annoying insect.

"She can be enthusiastic, too much. Have you lost your hand?"

As Wesley wrapped his handkerchief around it, some blood showed through. Between them the dog leaned forward panting, its tongue hanging out.

To Wesley, there was not a problem here. He looked at her. "Who are you?"

Serbian, Greek or even Russian; a long way from English, in every sense. And then there was her voice.

"This is my dog."

"I mean, are you—who?"

What? It wasn't clear even to him what he wanted to know. It was as if they both expected him to say something offhand and amusing—about rabies, for example; he could always try a mock fainting fit, going cross-eyed before collapsing in a heap on the footpath. But he wasn't much given to performance, seeing the funny side, coming out with one-liners; it had never become established in him. "You have an open relationship with blood," it occurred to him. "Whereas the men, we haven't." Something along those lines.

She'd given hardly a glance at his hand.

"I don't think you need to call an ambulance," he said, without meaning to be funny.

They had coffee and another one in a café. Those slightly dissatisfied eyes were a bit of a worry. Wesley thought she was in her late thirties. Afterwards, he went into the post office, which meant he had to explain to her the airmail envelopes. It allowed him to describe the working dogs on their sheep station. While he was at it he mentioned his sister, and that their mother had recently died.

Although she had declared herself a married woman she took him back to her place. This was a tall white house just down the road, at the left side of a small garden square, the very house—according to the plaque above the burglar alarm—where one of the greatest early Australian explorers had lived, which is what Wesley called himself, or rather made tender reference to, after removing her tracksuit. It was enough to prompt in this stout healthy woman, whose expression normally didn't vary much, shudderings of almost laughter.

After many afternoons spent in the house, Wesley Antill forgot which hand had been bitten, and at odd moments would examine the palms of each hand and flex the fingers unnecessarily.

Eventually he asked, "Did your dog actually take a bite out of me, or not?"

Wesley refrained from asking too many questions. The less he knew about her increased the chance of thinking clearly. And she didn't seem to mind his apparent lack of curiosity. She knew it would end soon. It was all it was.

One afternoon she sat up and said her husband had come home early, and straight out of an Ealing comedy Antill made his way out the back gate to the lane, where he hobbled into his shoes and trousers. A minor incident really, yet it could have turned nasty. It made Antill ask what he was doing with himself, how was he spending his time—was he being serious?

It was the solitude of a large city. And all he was doing was exploring, or rather, allowing. Antill understood he didn't need to be with anybody. Aspects of his character he preferred to keep to himself, without always knowing what they really were. In the same way he rarely mentioned his thoughts. So much of talking was for the sake of talking, just because somebody else happened to be talking, of obeying some necessary instinct to fill in the gaps, to add to what already had been said, or wanting to toss in a joke or a related anecdote to bring the house down (since only an infinitesimal amount of what is said is memorable). For hour after hour Antill practiced sitting in his room, emptying his mind of all thoughts. Preparing his mind for something: it was beginning to feel like that. To make matters worse, the room had just two sticks of furniture, a chair and a small brown-stained table. A smoker had been the previous tenant, and the pale shape of a crucifix showed where it had been hanging on a nail on the darkened wall.

Lindsey forwarded a letter from Rosie Steig, still at the same address in Sydney. It was soon afterwards on the footpath that Wesley began his conversations with the local postman, who did his rounds on foot, "single-handed delivery," as he put it, if rather ponderously, which became for Wesley necessary daily conversations. Looking out from his window at the crescent he waited for the tall figure in uniform to appear at one end, where he'd go down and join him and walk alongside for the remainder of the round, happy to let the postman do the talking. Wesley had never seen a postman as tall as the one he got to know in London, Lyell, and who not only talked but talked like a fast-dripping tap, when most other postmen were not talkers at all—the very opposite, in fact—despite, or perhaps because of, spending their working days hand-delivering words. Sometimes the pressure showed. There are the regular court cases where a postman of mild appearance has been found guilty of accumulating in his bedroom thousands of unopened letters he was supposed to have delivered. In Sydney, on Macleay Street, the aging postie, Brian, wore navy shorts in summer and winter, and had a cigarette, even in heavy April rain; a figure sloping forward, listening to the cricket on a transistor hidden in amongst the envelopes. If you were lucky he might give a nod, or "morning," nothing more.

Wesley noticed how Lyell had to concentrate, or enter some sort of mechanical groove, combining numbers with hand movements, as he moved from one address to the next, while his other thinking self continued doing the talking. He was a "career postman," he said, without smiling. "Drop these in 23." Unlike the specious opinions given all too freely by taxi drivers, which are seized upon as gospel by visiting journalists all over the world, as if the world can ever be seen and summarized through a windscreen, Lyell gave no opinions, except to declare early on he was a lucky man, his job was the best in the world. "Here I am," passing an aerogram to Wesley for delivery, "under the open sky talking to you. And getting paid for it." Coming out with short statements, what appeared to be aphorisms, was the closest he got to giving an opinion, imperfect, unpolished, incomplete. They were descriptions—of what he saw before him, ordinary objects.

A broken dining chair had been abandoned on the footpath; Lyell recalled in detail the different chairs he had owned, and others he remembered sitting on that he hadn't owned. His parents' rose-patterned armchair had a special width. Creaking, sighing, rustling, nothing—the different noises made by chairs. Often he could remember the chair, but not the person sitting on it. Those plump upholstered ones were indented with buttons like his aunt Sharon's navel (he had once blundered into her bedroom when she was standing naked). One Easter Friday he saw a street fight in Notting Hill between two West Indians using steel chairs. This soliloquy to the chair lasted for most of the round. The next morning he continued, having remembered a few more. "I have fond memories of all chairs."

People's different handwriting—another subject. And the names people give their poor children, as shown on the envelope, look. A man coming towards them reminded Lyell of his brother. He described his puffed-out cheeks, his vegetarian pallor, small ears, small hands, his sensitivity to cold, a carpenter who attended the cream-brick church of some sort of sect, married with three sons, the youngest suffering from a helpless stammer. As the postman talked he handed items of mail to Antill for hand-delivery, who still listening took quick strides down to a basement in amongst the cats and rubbish bins, or else up steps three at a time to the horizontal brass slot in a door. Together they finished the round early, and had their cup of tea in the Shepherd's Bush fish café, the one with the perspiring window.

Lyell talked about the other postmen. According to him, many were philosophers. One in particular could quote from "Mister Plato," almost off by heart, the way devoted Christians can reel off entire chapters from the Bible, and Muslims too, from their book. Another one—thin long hair tied in a ponytail—collected scarce editions of D. H. Lawrence after picking up a copy of *The Rainbow* in the gutter. Poets were a source of philosophy. A number of postmen were writers of poetry. While making deliveries, they could be seen moving their lips and frowning, so he informed Wesley, which meant they were composing as they walked. Others he had known were experts on the great describers, such as William Wordsworth; a New Zealander had introduced them to James K. Baxter—a poet who had himself been a postman in Wellington!

Although Antill didn't need to work he gave serious thought to becoming a postman.

Those mornings on the streets, and at his elbow the tall, perspiring, talkative postman handing him letters and small parcels at irregular intervals, in order to continue talking, or rather make his detailed description of things, went on for many months. Wesley was vaguely aware of being attracted to extremists.

The example set daily by the methodical postman encouraged an early return to thinking. Rather than a random searching-around, Wesley saw in the patchwork of descriptions a firm base—fit words only to what can be seen. It was a simple enough edict; one that was always there.

At the window he was anticipating as usual what the postman would kick off talking about. "Come on, Lyell." He glanced at his watch. His friend was never late.

A smaller figure appeared at the opening of the crescent, bending forward at each address, then jerking back, as if on strings. He had none of Lyell's unconscious fluency.

Wesley met him in the street—a thin West Indian wearing tan shoes with his uniform.

"They have sent him packing," he explained in a loud voice. "He has gone. Someone around here was reported doing his work for him, against all regulations written down. Excuse me now."

Of the so-called London years, only a few of the many hundreds of people he encountered had left an impression. He passed through them, as he did situations—passed through, came out from. And it was similar for those passing people. If one of them was told Wesley Antill from Sydney, who they met or slept with on such and such a day, had turned into a philosopher, those who remembered him at all would have been amazed. With men especially he left little or no trace.

His way of "thought-making," own description, was to continue wandering and take in. Remain open and fill in emptiness. On the train to Bath, a young Frenchman with a violin case on his knees spoke of the conversion of nature into art. Art, being human, is imperfect—hence, its power, smiled the Frenchman. Antill enjoyed the conversation, and thought of seeing more of him, perhaps becoming friends, but when it came to it he couldn't find his address. Women were like small towns: to come upon them, and be surrounded by their neatness, but without the help of directions, before reaching unexpected dead ends; and begin all over again, elsewhere. Beyond the Cotswolds there, she was quieter than a town, and modest, a trim village in white with a curve and a fork in the main street, where the hand came forward requesting an outsider to slow down, or even stop altogether, which is exactly what she did to him. There was confusion all round. Light-hearted women, waiting to laugh; plenty of others not so trusting; men bobbing up with their faulty jokes, quips, football scores and eye-rolls—before going off by themselves.

In London, at Kentish Town, he took a job at night cleaning schools, not for the money. He felt like using his hands. Out of the textbook, alongside "ferryman," he became a gardener for a large dark-stoned church and its manse, a good twenty miles from Ledbury. Weeds had taken over the church cemetery. After two world wars the spread of gravestones had almost surrounded the church. As he weeded, he saw the short, slow movements of remembrance. Old people and their neat hats, the small bunch of flowers. His other duties included sitting in the front pew and listening as the minister rehearsed Sunday's sermon. "Tell me, yes. And don't spare the horses. Feedback is what I require." Followed by tea.

The theological discussions were not satisfactory. Between taking calls the good distracted Presbyterian had no curiosity beyond the domination of one idea. A full schedule of small events may have helped. Wesley felt pity for his silent wife.

In work clothes Antill felt clumsy. Not only his hands, his thoughts—they were becoming blunt. And he was trying to make sense of it all, of what came towards him, of what he was part of. One difficulty was his separateness from nearby people. Everybody had this in different degrees; he knew that love can reduce the gap, almost to nothing. As he grew older he felt his separateness widen, slightly, but enough, as if the irreducible spaces between things in the wide-open landscape he grew up in had infected him, which he saw as a source of strength. In women, he sought—he wasn't sure what.

A movement somewhere was hardly possible without an alteration somewhere else. Do as little as possible? To his sister and Rosie Steig he described his various careers. In London, he volunteered for a soup kitchen operating near one of the arches of Charing Cross. Museum attendant: another possibility.

Both women, separately, rebuked him; he was wasting himself, as he surely could see. In consecutive postcards illustrating local characteristics (Tudor cladding, young lass holding basket of apples, Blackpool on a sunny day), he explained to Rosie he could no longer think constantly, even if he wanted to; and since he couldn't, he might as well work with his hands. He had avoided cities renowned for their philosophers, he told Rosie. In London, ordinary people on the street were philosophers without knowing it. Perhaps they pointed to a way, he told her. He made promises, then broke them.

21

ERICA HAD breakfast alone, a "thoughtful breakfast."
Roger Antill had already gone. His breakfast things were
in the sink. Off to see his girlfriend in town, was Erica's
thought, without first considering the nearby and distant
tasks awaiting the grazier that allow him to get out of the
house. Erica wondered how anyone could have such casual unconcern for the condition of their face. (In contrast
to his orderly hair.) With a countryman, the radiations of
kindliness spread-eagling from the eyes, known as "crow's
feet," are more likely to come from squinting daily into the
sun, wind and rain than laughing, let alone smiling all the
time. And this Roger's relaxed manner with women might
have to do with not actually caring about them much. Be
polite; that was about it.

Like her brother, Lindsey rose early. She could be heard
moving about; yet she rarely made an appearance before
seven thirty. Sophie was the late riser, a "night-person"
often missing breakfast altogether, just coffee.

Erica headed for the woolshed. There it stood, gray
iron, shining moisture. And clean cold air smoothed her
skin. She turned. Before her was the trouser-khaki dryness
stained with trees, with shadows ink spilt, a general elonga-
tion, rising and falling to the horizon, where it blurred to
mauve, one part lit up by sunlight. The women were in the
house soft in their early morning warmth; Mr. Roger Antill

out and about somewhere would be back for lunch or tea. And she had all morning in the quiet shed to immerse herself in the pages of philosophy. From every direction, even from faraway Sydney, she felt a flow of anticipatory happiness, so unusual, faint yet strong, she stopped everything and opened her mouth to preserve it.

When she pushed open the door to the shed, the draft fluttered some of the pages. Erica went forward and sat at the table where Antill sat, surrounded by papers. This time she noticed more pages cascading from the horsehair sofa. She felt others underfoot and bent down and gathered them up. It was a matter of where to begin. Unless Antill's philosophical investigations consisted of nothing but lengthy hesitations, or digressions coming to a grinding halt, or scraps, or notes. To stumble across a full-blown, assembled dissertation, complete in its sweep and conclusions, if such a thing was ever possible, would make the journey from Sydney and the time spent well worthwhile. Here it all was—in front of her. As far as Erica was concerned, there was an honorable history of uncompleted philosophical works, not to mention complete U-turns. She could not avoid thinking of her own work.

Antill's writing was large, plain and tilted, with many additions, crossings out, circles, arrows, asterisks. Ink was added to pencil, and vice versa. It was hard to read. And while the other pages on the shelves were in rectangular piles of different heights, like an architect's model for a dream city consisting entirely of skyscrapers, these pages half stacked and scattered on the table suggested Antill had been working on them the day he died. They were dog-eared from constant handling, with a splash on one of the pages Erica assumed was tomato sauce.

She went over to the shelves and turned over other pages to see if the writing was any better. These were in blue ink—and had just as many scratched-out lines and altered paragraphs, additions, circles, "a real dog's breakfast," Roger Antill would say. So far as she could tell the rest were also in ink.

Back in the chair, Erica glanced up at the notes Antill had written to himself and pegged on the length of string, *a kind of involuntary and unconscious memoir, yes,* and *priest of nature.* Next to it was a quote she didn't recognize, *To Be There and To Wonder.* Perhaps it was Antill's own.

She spread out the pages, and settled down to read his words.

Erica saw in "To Be There and To Wonder" a personal statement. It was experience turned into a proposition, certainly worth consideration, to recognize further, but not now.

She returned to the page.

"I realized in Germany with R, or even before in my London years, when I avoided all thinking—and following the visit to Amsterdam, where I deliberately placed myself in a philosophical city, I realized after the visit of R, and the unwanted experience of tragedy, it was necessary to—"

Here Erica frowned. Where was the philosophy? Skipping ahead, all she found was the continuing story of his life—evidently Antill believed it to be more important than philosophy—unless he was following Descartes' momentous example, snowbound in Germany. Or else the hardcore philosophy Erica had been hired to appraise was in the blue-ink pages on the horsehair sofa, the shelves, and even scattered on the floor.

Sophie came into the shed, holding a mug of coffee.

"I need to talk to you."

If Erica had turned she would have noticed her friend without makeup, and irregular red patches on her cheeks.

"Look at this." Erica waved an arm which took in the pages on the table, and the rest fluttering on the shelves and floor. "It's going to take many moons before I make the slightest headway."

"How long has it gone on for?"

"What do you mean?"

Sophie put her mug on the table which allowed her to pace backwards and forwards.

"Do you think I'm blind? Think I'm completely stupid? I saw the way you talked on the telephone. He wanted to talk to you, not me. Just tell me. I'd really like to know. Tell me."

Erica turned.

"Of the available men in Sydney, you have to sleep with him. He is my father, in case you've forgotten. How long for? Who seduced who?"

"Since before Christmas," Erica murmured.

"Thank you very much. That's all I need."

Sophie had her face turned from Erica, then she looked up at the ceiling.

"I don't know why I am talking to you. Do you have any idea what this is going to do to me?"

As Erica went to touch her arm, Sophie reared back, knocking the coffee over. In a fast wave it engulfed the handwritten pages arranged for Erica's scrutiny.

Erica stood up. "Look what you've done!"

"What you've done," Sophie turned away.

Erica could only stare at the spreading mess.

"A handkerchief, or something, quick."

There was nothing handy. Removing her blouse, Sophie threw it on the pages, already saturated pale brown.

Erica tried to soak it up and at the same time pick up sheets to save.

"This is terrible, I don't know what to do."

Most of the pages were ruined.

"Oh who cares? And anyway what has wonderful 'philosophy' done for you?"

"Sleeping with your strong, rich-with-words, always attentive father for one," Erica almost shouted. "And what has psychoanalysis, therapy and all the rest of it done for your life? Has it made you a better person?"

Erica felt she had lost control.

"I'm going to start screaming."

Already Sophie was asking herself whether the accident was willed. The subconscious is said to be responsible for many such interventions. Outside, in the sunlight, bare-skinned in her skirt without a blouse, like an island woman who had been forced by missionaries into wearing a brassiere, she wondered if and when—and how—she should confront her father. Who seduced who? Then why should it matter—so much? Sophie paused and thought of going back. Helping Erica clean up would too easily be seen as giving support.

A complete and utter disaster: it went directly against her principles, her beliefs.

Erica had a dogged loyalty to fellow-thinkers, whoever they were, whatever the quality.

She had her head down using her fingernails to separate the wet pages and place them on the floor to dry; and as they dried she saw the brown stain had wiped out the urgent additions in Mediterranean blue and the page numbers in ink too. The terrible incident—it was an accident!—had left her feeling wrung out. She still couldn't believe the suddenness of it. She was going to have dreams about this. A man's lifework ruined; made a mockery of; and in one movement the very reason for her being there, in the solitude of the philosopher's shed, ruined.

Because Erica had done nothing wrong she could not bear to face the others at lunch. To Lindsey, she would soon have to explain and apologize. As for Sophie, Erica had no idea what she would say to her now—exactly what expression should she keep on her face?

By three o'clock Erica was still in Antill's chair, surrounded by the damage.

There was the other Antill, Roger, and she heard him come into the shed.

Without turning she said, "I've had a truly terrible morning. And it began so perfectly."

Roger stood still surveying the mess which was a country flood in miniature.

Before he could say anything she said, "I am sorry. Look at it. Did Sophie tell you?"

"I haven't seen the others," he said.

"Ruined. Unreadable. I don't know what to say."

"What about all them?" He went over to the shelves and turned a few pages. "It looks like philosophy to me. How about this? *Life is the intruder on thought.*" Roger Antill laughed, a soft, internal, stifled laugh of appreciation. "That sounds like my brother. And you could say that's what's happened here. What was it—weak coffee?"

Still with his back to her, he flipped over some of the other pages.

"There's plenty for you to make an appraisal. Something out of all this could be worth printing into a book."

"I haven't taken a close look over there yet."

"Wesley putting his thoughts on paper wrote furiously. He used to sit here with his boiled eggs."

Roger Antill still had his stockman's hat on; plus shirt of faded broad-check pattern, blue and black-blue, sleeves rolled up.

"I've lost count of the schooners and cups of tea, vases of Lindsey's flowers and whatnot I've made a mess of in my time. Not long ago it was a drum of sheep dip on the front seat of the car. It went everywhere."

Erica listened. Occasional male kindness came across as different from the kindness of women. It was a practical, offhand kindness. There was always the slightly puffy, rough-skinned slippage of her father's hand—lasting assumptions held in the palm of a hand.

Walking amongst the drying pages he reached across the table and found one of the few readable ones.

"Let's see what Wesley's got to say." His eyes followed a few lines, then cleared his throat.

"'In Zoellner's bookshop in Amsterdam, along Rosemarijnsteeg, where I had earlier lost my temper and was forced to leave, I met and became friends with Carl and George Kybybolite—the extravagant, insistent individuality of Americans and their surnames—brothers from Chicago. Their education was formal. They were big men in untidy clothes. Both had loud and confident voices. They were a double-act; each finished the other's sentences. When they heard my reason for being in Holland, and my background of farming in Australia, it was Carl, the quicker of the two, who called me 'the Cartesian bore.'"

"That's funny," Erica acknowledged. "That's very funny," she sparked up. Though she still felt gutted.

"Not bad," Roger turned the page over, "I'd like to read more. Wesley did take himself seriously. When he came back, and set himself up here, he had nothing but blank pages, reams of the stuff. Early on he wanted to show me what he had written. I'd take a deep breath, and say to him he had too many ideas running off in every direction, in each sentence. To show what I meant, I'd point to the sheep in the yards: they're made to go through a narrow space, one at a time, not all at once. 'Thanks for that,' my brother said. He was sitting in that same chair looking at me. 'I'm going to bear that in mind.'"

Erica moved from the table.

"What I suggest we do now," he almost put his hand on her hip, "is, I go and make you a cup of tea. Leave all this. It's still going to be here tomorrow."

22

——I REALIZED in Germany with R, or even before in my London years, when I avoided all *thought-thinking*—my incessant movements were to avoid thinking—and following the visit to Amsterdam, where I deliberately placed myself in the midst of a philosophical city, I realized after the visit of R, and the unwanted experience of tragedy, it was necessary to build on what I had learnt and to make up for lost time. How old was I then? Forty-three. What did I know? How could I describe what I had learnt?

It is very easy to become sick and tired of "philosophy."

The very word is enough to send a normal person running in the opposite direction.

The ambition to supply the answer to everything is a form of madness. It can lead to the kissing of a broken-down horse on a street in Turin. The lives of the philosophers. Those who went to extreme political positions. The suicides. One is supposed to have died from "malnutrition." Their silences, et cetera. "I do not wish to know if there were men before me." Unquote.

Philosophy is not necessarily a safe occupation.

All day sitting in a chair, alone. The process of venturing into the outer limits of thought can produce—it is only natural—psychological distortions well beyond any eccentric behavior.

But then my brother, Roger, running the sheep station in New South Wales, faces dangerous situations every day of his life, in all weathers. Tractors end up rolling over onto the farmer; branches from the Brittle Gum break and fall onto them; head-ons with trucks, stray stock and trees are common on country roads; Roger broke his collarbone off a horse; he is probably now riddled with melanoma.

In Europe I wrote regularly to Roger, and my sister, Lindsey, who has the long face, and although my brother only occasionally replied I felt the need to write more frequently the longer I was away. I realize now my letters and postcards were nothing more than the banal descriptions of another tourist. I assumed it would be the only thing of interest to them, the only information they could handle, nothing more than descriptions, easily digested. "Berlin has been largely rebuilt since the war. It is a city of many small courtyards, gardens and greenery. It is late September and everybody is in shirtsleeves." If they had seen through the ordinariness of my messages they didn't let on. After many years away, doing nothing of a practical nature, their belief in me was deep and true.

On the morning following my return I sat them down in the kitchen and explained what I would like to do. It would depend on them. The word "sacrifice" was used quite easily. I wanted two undisturbed years to complete my philosophical work. It could go to three. Lindsey sat looking at me, already nodding encouragement, while Roger kept getting up for a glass of water, or taking a look out the window at the weather, and sitting down.

I have always had trouble working out who I am. All I have is a faint idea of what I am not.

In an effort to avoid the simplicities I complicate my thoughts and speech.

"If that's what you want," Roger said from the window. "I'd say you know what you're doing. You're onto something, are you?"

No sooner had they agreed than I removed their permission from my mind.

——FINALLY, I left England (October 3, 1988). By then I felt separate from the majority of other people—because

I had moved my thoughts well away from their thoughts. And living in a foreign place, such as England, is already to experience daily a *double*-separateness. I had in the winter returned to libraries, attracted by the central heating, and began rereading. It was necessary to begin all over again. Those years in England without reading and without thinking had done no harm at all. I felt fresh. I was ready. The sight of people in Hyde Park resting in rented deck chairs left a poor impression on me. I remember at the Ritz end, a middle-aged man in a fine hound's-tooth and a carnation in the lapel attempting to get out of his deck chair, the trouble he had extricating himself, like a nation trying to regain prestige, or a thinker trying to get out from under the weight of the past. There and then I decided it was time to leave England and the sensible, comparatively decent English, and, before returning home, subject myself to Europe.

If I had stayed in London another week I would have stayed for the rest of my life.

On the ferry to Calais with very little luggage I felt an eagerness verging on the ecstatic. Only rarely have I experienced this. It was mid-morning. I had the day spread out before me, as if it was being opened by stage curtains. Within a few hours I'd be stepping ashore on a strange land, performing on a strange stage. And I saw my remaining life spreading outwards, and beckoning with hints and promises of clarity.

I opened my notebook. When the ferry began pitching and rolling, which frightened some of the girls into shrieking, others going quiet, I concentrated on my thoughts. Traversing liquid that separates the land is curious when considered dispassionately. We are on earth and making the best of it. (I thought I might begin from there.)

Facing me sat a neat, silent couple, holding hands. He was old enough to have a purple face; she, hardly twenty. I soon found out he was deaf.

He was a pig farmer from Somerset. He was going to inspect some French pigs, and was taking his new wife along for a break. "I don't fancy leaving her behind. What do you say?"

As I looked at her, she smiled a fraction and remained looking at me. What is going on here? Either she is as innocent as her complexion, or else she is marrying for convenience. As the purple-faced farmer told me in a loud voice everything I needed to know about pigs and their intelligence, I could not help trying to unravel what attracted me to the women I had known, in many ways different from each other, when others did not possess the power of attraction at all. Any thoughts I may have had of a philosophical nature were hampered by this, along with the steady buildup of solid information on pigs and ham coming from the farmer, and disturbed still further by the unshakable gaze of his young wife. She had never been out of England before, she confided, in fact, only out of the Somerset district for one afternoon.

"In France you're not going to know the name of things," I pointed out. It sounded as if I was offering translation services. I remember feeling lighthearted.

The farmer didn't appear to notice.

"It's business in Germany, I expect?" They both looked at me.

"I'd like to see for myself the white swans," I explained.

Swans—that was a mistake. Even the slightly plump, pleasure-loving wife began laughing as the farmer switched his information-flow to his experience of swans, followed by geese.

The ferry plowed on descending into the troughs, banging and rattling. I realized I had never been on open water before. It was raining. Nothing much to see.

If I happened to be passing through Strasbourg early in the week, it was agreed I would call on them; which I did, out of extreme curiosity, and on the second day spent an afternoon alone with her, Gretel, in my hotel.

——THE PHILOSOPHERS have been unsatisfactory in the examination of the emotions. To be expanded upon later.

Already I forget the blasted name of the former fishing village near Collioure, the one where I had a cheese sandwich in the square. I sat in the sun and began writing to Roger and Lindsey. The postcards here showed painted wooden boats pulled up on the beach.

To Rosie, I wrote a letter of several pages. I described the ferry, and my encounter with Gretel, and left it at that. Often I thought of Rosie. What I could not fathom was her informality. Even when being kind, or loyal, or passionate it was done without reason, as if she would give the same to others. In this letter I said how much I missed her, and wished she were here. "Braque spent his summers in this fishy village, which meant Picasso probably did too," I wrote knowingly.

Men in the square were happily playing *boule* in the face of their fast-approaching deaths. (My initial thoughts.) And yet they were engrossed. Friendship played a part in the game. They all knew each other. Their skill, and undoubted pleasure at their skill, gave precision to their friendships, and drew me into watching them.

At the next table was a Greek in a white shirt.

"Many mustaches," he nodded at the players.

He was right. They all had mustaches. And when I turned I saw he had a black one too.

In front of us the local fire brigade assembled for a parade. As they formed up in lines the ill-fitting uniforms became all too apparent—trousers above the ankles, like those worn by shearers' cooks—and brass buttons missing. An implacable figure who looked to be the local mayor gave a short speech, and as he did members of the brigade winked and stuck their tongues out at people they knew in the crowd. Stepping forward for presentations a thin-necked one played the clown.

"The only fire they've seen would be from their cigarette lighters." Another pessimistic Greek.

A band started up. The fire brigade marched off.

In the evening the Greek was at the same table. He recommended the sardines.

He came from Melbourne. Now he was a waiter on a cruise ship, and lived in Piraeus. It had become necessary to take a holiday. He'd left the wife and kids behind in Piraeus. As marriages go it was okay, but he was dog-tired. To save washing up on the ship, he said later in the evening, they would toss the dinner plates over into the Mediterranean.

"The ocean floor's covered in the bloody plates."

This was something to tell Lindsey, my easily horrified sister. I even thought of waiting until I returned—to see the look on her face.

To give proper homage to philosophy I had been planning to return home via Athens.

"It is the arsehole of the universe. There is nothing to be said for Athens. It is ugly, dusty, crowded—a bloody mess. What do you want to go there for? It is a ruined city."

The Parthenon stands above the shambles as an example, a rebuke. Clive Renmark at the lectern had said as much. The ancient philosophers looking down would recoil. How a city of ideals became a graceless dump. Everybody out for themselves. The wisdom of the greatest of philosophers is consumed, whittled away, ignored, cast on the rubbish tip like everything else. Their ideals of proportion and harmony not only ignored, scorned. A friend had told the postman, Lyell, the same thing.

Every night the Greek ended up pissed. That was all right. More difficult was the man's encroaching pessimism. It reached out to most things he saw or touched, and sitting there alongside it was all too easy to join in.

Early in the morning I left on the bus. In Toulon, I wolfed down a breakfast of bread and jam, coffee in a bowl. I then strolled over and studied the map on the wall of the railway station.

My method of wandering in Europe had returned to being haphazard, hardly a method at all. Depending on mood, chance encounters were to be seized upon. Otherwise, what is the point—in living? So I thought then. If and when I was onto something with my thinking-notes I would stop and stay in one spot. It also allowed me to collect letters from Rosie, and my hardworking brother and sister. (For all the familiarity it is hard to reduce the distance between brothers.) In Europe I developed the insistence on second-floor corner rooms. It got to the stage that if there was not one available I'd move to another hotel. From two angles of a corner room I could look down at the traffic and pedestrians, and across at the lighted windows opposite. I felt at home—and in a strange country.

At the Kunstmuseum in Basel I stood for hours before Holbein's rotting (my opinion) Christ. Eventually the attendant got up from his wooden chair and joined me, and after a respectful silence asked me what I liked about it.

"It's a landscape. The elongated composition—the yellowing body—a land suffering, a drought landscape." I rattled on, "I know land like it. It's got nothing to do with Christ."

Later, at a museum specializing in 20th-century art, I came across a painting of black lines on gray by Mondrian, done in 1912. I stepped forward to read the label: *Eucalyptus*. I reared back. It was the last thing I wanted to see. Here I have traveled thousands of miles by plane, rail, bus, ferry and by foot, only to be presented in Switzerland with a painted version of something common I had left well behind. What would a Dutchman know about eucalypts? I imagined the artist with a brush in his hand. Mondrian was trying to make a virtue out of the tree's untidiness— branches and dead sticks hanging and drooping, or else shooting out all over the place. It was a pretty poor imitation. I remember on a train in England a Frenchman telling me the problem for the landscape painter was deciding what to leave out.

Rosie would like a postcard of it. I couldn't imagine what Roger would make of it.

Whether it was seeing Mondrian's messy painting, or writing the New South Wales address on the postcards, or the postcards of the painting combined with the Holbein "landscape," or what—for the first time I had thoughts of returning home. It was about time I stayed in the one spot.

I would pass through Amsterdam, quickly gather my thoughts in Germany.

——How to avoid becoming blunt and plain-thinking again. It happened if and when a stranger spoke to me on a train, in a park, on a bridge. Once having spoken—where do I go from here?

It had become part of my blundering about. Watch it! Little point visiting Prague. After a day I left. The river rushing through the center of Geneva—cold and bottle-green. It continually carried history along with it (history from I don't know where—from other countries?). To stand on one of the bridges, looking down, drew me into the flow and the flow of time, and quite separate the flow of consciousness which passes at a steady rate through us. While considering this, I didn't notice any of the locals leaning over the bridge, lost in thought.

It is a struggle.

At any given moment there are signals, movements, metal and flesh, temperatures, opinions of others, corrections, differences of time, and other obscurities competing for our impressions. How to make sense of it; what to avoid (like the painter of landscapes).

Almost everything seen will be forgotten. Very little of what I saw did I actually experience.

On a canal in northern France a small girl on a barge was going higher and higher on a swing set up by her father, a carefree, semicircular movement in contrast to the horizontal forward movement of the barge. Why this insignificant image has remained is beyond me. To any beggar holding out their hand I gave a coin. (That's something in my day you didn't often see in Australia—beggars.) The town of two rivers. So I turned to the man in the bus. "It is more than twice as interesting." As for me, the ancient stone bridges are an impediment. On the footpath outside the bar in view of the container docks, Rotterdam, I looked on as three men in orange boilersuits fought with bottles, a matter of standing back and estimating their chances until the police arrived. Europe's systematic cultivation—the place has been leveled, squared up to within an inch of its life. The different densities of green. There's no such thing as a brown paddock. No sooner would I choose a café, and sit out in the sun to enjoy a ham or a cheese sandwich than I began thinking of the paddocks at home where not a thing moves. In these circumstances, as I sat and allowed my thoughts to focus, an English newspaper on my knee had more importance than it deserved.

When I arrived in Amsterdam I had real trouble finding a corner room on the second floor. It took me all morning, and then I had to pay over my budget—I recognized and admired my stubbornness. It was on one of the canals, the Hotel Brouwer. After putting my things on the bed, I set out to wander without any destination in mind.

That morning I saw two women crying. One riding a bicycle with a wicker basket in front almost ran me down. Tears were flowing from behind her granny glasses. She had taken no notice of me. I made a movement to help, or at least offer sympathy, but she was on her way. Not long after, near the Stedelijk Museum, where I had no intention of entering, I sat at one end of a bench, away from a middle-aged woman seated at the other end. Straightaway she began crying. A wide face, I saw, and a small mouth.

By leaning forward, more or less facing her, I gave the impression of a sympathetic figure. She might have glanced in my direction and nodded for help. Why, after all, begin weeping the minute I sat down? She went on weeping. I leaned back to my normal position believing it was possible to share without awkwardness the bench with an unhappy, exceptionally neat, middle-aged woman.

After a few minutes I opened my notebook. Jot down the fleeting thoughts, even those that don't appear important, in this case thoughts on the emotions. (The many different kinds of weeping. Tears and Natural Selection. Weeping is visual for the following reasons . . .)

It was then a younger woman in jeans and khaki waistcoat with bulging pockets stopped and aimed a camera at me. I realized the gap between me and the unhappy woman on the bench must have indicated a married couple drifting apart at the rate of knots. Obviously, I was the guilty party.

I stood up and waved my arms. I don't like to be photographed. To drive home the point I launched into a diatribe against photography, its self-importance, its essential shallowness, its melodramatic seriousness, the ridiculous impertinence of photographers, et cetera. I had a sudden urge to break open her camera.

Only when she said firmly but defensively, "Everybody has their photo taken today" did I realize she was Australian (Brisbane).

Not another tourist snapping at a picturesque scene, a serious photographer, an *artist-photographer* (her description) who exhibited in the museums, mostly in Australia. She did projects. These she constructed into exhibitions. The Amsterdam project, which included five other European cities, meant moving around with the camera, selecting people at random she imagined were Australian—only to discover most of them were Poles, Danes, Latvians, Italians, Canadians, British and even Icelandic. The idea being to demonstrate perceptions, habits, prejudices.

"Are you one? I thought you looked Australian or something."

Out of the corner of my eye, I saw the woman on the bench blowing her nose, adjusting her scarf.

"You have a British plum in your mouth. But your face—the jaw—shoulders," she went on, the perpetual photographer, "I think you're Australian!"

——UNTIL I MET the Kybybolite brothers, Carl and George, I intended staying only a day or two in Amsterdam. Lindsey and Rosie believed I was on my way home. I'd sent them a forwarding address in Berlin.

As well, I was ready to leave Amsterdam in a hurry because Cynthia Blackman had moved into my corner room with her camera gear—the rucksacks, aluminium cases. Almost immediately, she opened the window and proceeded to focus her long lens along the canal and bicycle tracks, and into parked cars, in the hope of coming across a rare and enduring image. Restless in a room, restless outside—alert, that's the better word. Enough to drive a man mad. While aiming the camera, Cynthia often swore. She had short black hair and dark eyes. I wouldn't say she was a happy person.

I agreed she could stay one night. But when she raised her T-shirt, again I was conscious of how the ordinary movements of life, offered here in the form of softness, shadow, warmth, invitation, pushed to one side all other thoughts, I mean my persistent philosophical thoughts, which have been a way of thinking I knew I could not avoid. The search for philosophical answers of any worth requires a certain remoteness from life. Keeping on the path is the difficulty. And there I was spending whole days and entire nights in pleasure with Cynthia Blackman.

She never went anywhere without one of her state-of-the-art cameras. Such was her alertness on the street I could only tag along in her wake. Anything I said didn't seem to register. Aside from concentration, this mode of working was part of imposing authority on any image, which was very important, she said (even though, I told myself, the image was already there).

I felt uncomfortable in public with Cynthia and her cameras. When she stopped in her tracks and took aim at an unsuspecting tourist I would turn and walk away—couldn't bear the association. It soon became a source of trouble between us.

Zoellner's was a bookshop on Rosmarijnsteeg. It sold nothing but books on philosophy. As soon as I went in and activated the little brass bell over the door I knew Cynthia waiting outside would become impatient. She was anxious to add more subjects to her Amsterdam project.

Spinoza was Zoellner's speciality. Other philosophers were stocked but, it was made plain enough, they were eunuchs at the feet of a giant. Spinoza took up an entire wall. Rare items were displayed in a cabinet, including a lock of his hair . . . Benedictus Spinoza is a very impressive figure, as far as I'm concerned. I came to him late. "Love and desire can be excessive." And he then went on to explain why. He also wrote strongly about things I had not experienced, such as hatred and fame.

Two Americans were talking and reaching out for books, turning a few pages by sliding their thumb down from the top right corner, before replacing them. Spinoza died at forty-four—consumption. Now three hundred years later, three men, four counting Zoellner, who sat at a ridiculously small desk, still found in the pages he wrote thoughts and reflections of worth.

It was in Zoellner's bookshop in Amsterdam that I realized I wanted to create a philosophy so I could die happily.

In a loud voice one of the Americans asked, "Do you happen to know where Spinoza lived in this town? Is the house still standing?"

Before the bookseller could answer, the brass bell above the door gave a tingle and Cynthia came in young, braless, and clearly not interested in books. As the Americans turned, and Zoellner looked up, she began snapping away with her camera.

The Americans were relaxed about photography, Zoellner was not.

Disconcerted, I found myself leaping in to defend photography, or Cynthia (since they were one and the same), who appeared unconcerned at the shouting. Zoellner had a black beard. He was a man in his sixties. Somehow he remained expressionless while raising his voice.

The origins of a hot temper are difficult to trace.

Out on the footpath the Kybybolite brothers hosed me down.

"Not exactly the Spinozan way of resolving matters," I remember one of them saying. "But, hell, don't go letting it bother you."

He went on to explain that spending every day for x number of years surrounded by the dense arguments and commentaries of the greatest thinkers, all turgidly or urgently—and cogently—put, had gone to his head (Zoellner's). Never mind the scholarly, dim-lit atmosphere. He made the point that secondhand book-dealers tend to be uncommercial bilious personalities, the complete opposite to those choosing the glossy environment of rows of gleaming new bestsellers.

We sat down in a café. They were big men, both of them. Always wearing the rough patterned shirt of the lumberjack. We joined them for breakfasts and dinners, and followed them to bars in suburbs almost but not quite off the beaten track. Together we took the train to The Hague to see the paintings. I had complained about Mondrian and his version of eucalypts. We had a good old time. It wasn't all lighthearted stuff. I had never before talked with anyone about philosophical matters. Carl and George both had attended the University of Chicago, and so spoke with an assured, almost breezy knowledge of the main achievements in Western philosophy. They finished each other's sentences. Carl, though, had become addicted to dropping in significant quotes of other thinkers, sometimes two or three in the one sentence, so that it became hard to know exactly what his own thoughts were. I caught myself grinning at their extraordinary New World informality when Carl, in particular, identified quotes by the philosopher's Christian name—"What Immanuel came up with . . ." or, "An aim is servitude, as Friedrich would say" or, "Consider for a second Ludwig's . . ." and, "The Bishop got it wrong, that's for sure."

Although I had barely been ten minutes in Zoellner's bookshop, and a few weeks in the company of Carl and George, it was in Amsterdam that I began positioning myself. I could feel it. I was beginning to gather my ideas. And I resolved to send Zoellner a copy of my philosophy, when it was printed (and to Carl and George, as well).

Already Carl was about to publish his own thesis, *The Science of Appearances*—if I remember correctly. Nothing to do with photography, George gave Cynthia a nudge. She enjoyed their company. He and Cynthia used to joke at my expense.

I could feel within myself a beneficial hardening. It was a foretaste of clarity. No doubt it made me solemn, stolid even, for I didn't talk much. By contrast the Kybybolite brothers were playful. They took Cynthia to films.

It was my continuing education.

—— Lindsey wrote to say our father was ill.

I telephoned. My sister sounded matter-of-fact about our father. He was almost in the past. Of closer interest was when I was coming home, and was I eating properly? Had I fallen for a Dutch woman? She put Roger on and he too shouted, as if our family were barbarians, "When are we seeing you back here?"— an interesting variation on, "When are you coming home?"

Eventually, when I spoke to my father it sounded as if he didn't recognize me, and could not fit the voice to the face. It was no use. Suddenly he mentioned in very clear terms a stamp-dealer in London I should visit, "a decent individual." Then he lapsed again, making no sense.

23

It is clear that ordinary subjects can acquire powers through special usage, and adjust their shape, or else we do, until they become extensions of our selves. The modest couch Freud employed in Vienna which had a central part in his treatment of, or listening to, hysterics became endowed with mystical qualities—the couch to which all others are compared. It should come as no surprise that when Freud in the nineteen-thirties fled to London he was accompanied by the beetroot-colored couch with its Austro-Hungarian tassels and fringes, and set it against the wall in his consulting room in Hampstead, just as a concert pianist can only play on his particular Steinway, which may be fifty or sixty years old, and not always in tune.

Meanwhile, many photographs exist of philosophers half-reclining in deck chairs. Not merely the British philosophers shown at leisure amongst the dons in flannels on one of the back lawns of Cambridge, or at a 45-degree angle puffing the pipe on the outer of the Bloomsbury group, which is another part of the deck chair story, or the picture we have handed down of Wittgenstein's room where the only piece of furniture was a deck chair. There's a shot taken through a telephoto lens of Martin Heidegger relaxing in what looks like a deck chair, outside the hut at Todtnauberg. It's him, all right—though barely visible. These slack canvas chairs suspend like a drop of water just above the grass. They are closer to the earth than other chairs. Two people cannot share one. They are difficult things to get out of. The philosopher tries a few different deck chairs until settling on one that fits his shape.

24

IN THE KITCHEN Erica sat with Roger at the long table. It was the room she liked best. From here people fanned out in all directions to continue their daily tasks, while the scrubbed table, chairs, cream-fronted stove and black kettle remained in fixed positions, waiting on their return. Erica poured the tea for Roger, as her mother did for her father when he came home from work.

Roger Antill sat easily. It was his world. He was running the show. So he kept glancing out the window, one eye on the weather or whatever. As a rule, Roger didn't mind if and when a gap opened in the conversation, and remained open, even if—or especially—with a woman, a city-woman he hardly knew. It would never occur to him to rush in ad-libbing. Better to sit back. In these circumstances he allowed his mind to wander into something altogether different from the woman-problem at his elbow. Grass was growing in the paddocks, and sheep loaded down with wool were multiplying. The stationary engine needed loading onto the truck and taken into town. He glanced at Erica and almost smiled at how she was slightly overdressed for the district. With her head unnaturally bowed he could without being sprung take his time noticing her neck, vulnerable in its trusting curve and suggestion of hair which parted the way wind can leave a furrow in grass.

"I have to tell you," Erica turned as Lindsey came in. "There's been coffee spilt all over your brother's pages. Ruined. I don't know what to do."

Lindsey sat opposite.

"How did this happen?"

Normally at this point Roger would pick up his hat and leave.

"There's still plenty to go on," he said to his sister. "I wouldn't get too worried."

Erica shook her head. "I suspect those pages were important. They were the ones on his desk."

Lindsey poured herself tea.

"Then we shall see."

This was more sharp than thoughtful. Erica glanced at her. She's concerned about this more than her brother. He is kind to me.

Such "accidents" hardly ever happened to Erica. Her method of thinking reduced the chances of. But lately at work and with shopkeepers and fellow pedestrians she had been attracting misunderstanding, incidents, embarrassments, clumsy moments, confusions—the small awkwardnesses which of course represented something else. She preferred just then not to be in the welcoming kitchen— anywhere, but here. And yet, she wanted to stay. She could have screamed! Sophie, if she were there, would have spotted the tone and cut to the chase (professional habit), "Yes, but what do you *feel?*" Sophie was alert to the strength of feelings. Most days in her work she patiently sought in a person what was hidden. And she could never be sure whether or not anything was there, or worth retrieving, held up, isolated—or how long it would take to uncover. According to her father, Sophie had the life of a detective who never moved from the one room. Not meant unkindly; it allowed Erica to lean back in bed and laugh. They were in the Sundowner Motel.

Through the window Sophie now appeared on the veranda, pacing up and down, trying to work her mobile. And beginning with Roger they each paused to look at her.

"I'd better tell her," Roger stood up. "If it's Sydney she's trying to get, she could be in a spot of bother. But they're working on it," he said through his teeth.

From her hand luggage Sophie had managed to find a T-shirt in English mustard Erica hadn't seen before, chosen to display her figure to the full, and a filmy scarf with a few flowers as its feature. The trousers were burgundy linen, nicely cut. As if nothing had happened in the woolshed she waved, and signaled she was coming in.

Excusing herself, Erica stood up and went to her room.

It had been a mistake bringing Sophie along on this— just because she felt sorry for her. And typically she had preferred company to traveling alone into the interior, hundreds of miles west of Sydney. It was her timid side. What was the matter with her?

She stood at the bedroom window.

A return to her customary detachment was necessary. It was what she was known for.

Stepping outside, Erica went down towards the creek. Dozens of white cockatoos flew up from the ground ahead of her. There were other birds too, smaller birds. One had a short fan-shaped tail. The very idea of birds suddenly was amazing. Even crows. The many small, well-fitted bones. And two different lizards, one laughably plump, didn't bother to move. When she had been driving with Roger he cursed the rabbits. But here the sight of them excited her—their zigzag high speed.

The homestead and woolshed became smaller and smaller, until they disappeared.

Erica was stopping and sometimes squatted to examine all sorts of rocks, burrows (foxes), droppings (sheep, rabbits), animal trails, tufts of tough grass and the tiny flowers. Pale brown puddles of water reflected the clouds. A paddockful of sheep stopped and stared at her.

What possible dent could philosophy make on the fact of existence? The philosopher suffers from a rare disease of all-knowingness. Did Wesley know how to live? His dogged personality was oppressive. He was a tomato-sauce thinker. Look at the hundreds of handwritten pages stacked and overflowing in the all-gray corrugated iron shed. What a place to compose a meaningful slant. It was a hollow center.

Thinking of Roger, the brother left to work the property, she saw his uncommon generosity. It was associated with his smell, which she found attractive, male sweat, dug-up earth, actual wool, possibly his hair—the last man in Australia still using hair oil?

So Erica walked until the ground became steep and uneven, perforated with rabbit holes.

In sight of the homestead, Sophie came out to meet her. She put an arm around Erica's waist, which is how together they reached the veranda.

"I decided to go for a little walk."

"We were beginning to wonder . . ."

Erica's impulse was to consider the word "we."

"Have you spoken to Lindsey?"

"Look, something's done a little something on your shoulder. That's supposed to be good luck."

Licking her tiny handkerchief, Sophie held Erica's arm and rubbed it off.

"Are you regarding this as a bit of a holiday?" Sophie whispered. "I could almost learn to like it here, however much I'm not addicted to tea-drinking. Roger has to go into town in a minute. He's asked me to come for the ride. I could change, but this will do. What do you make of him? I'd say he's a hard one to read. There are men who are married to something solid, in his case it's the earth and the fences and everything."

Erica had been thinking she'd better tread warily with Lindsey. She was beginning to see she was not a happy woman—didn't know what was going on there. But now she became sharply irritated with Sophie, a woman who had always yawned at the very mention of the country. When it suited her, Sophie changed tack. She didn't live by rules, not even the rules of psychology, if there were any.

It sent Erica back to the calamity in the woolshed. And she felt a rush of coldness flow towards everyone.

No one was in the kitchen.

So Sophie said, "Listen, we have to talk."

Ever since they had known each other Sophie employed specialized energy-words to give her conversation, or rather the interrogations and summations, an emphatic clipped structure, never ordinary. These words included *indicative* and *in point of fact* and *practically*, and to offer nodding encouragement when talking to women, *exactly* and *precisely* or *I agree absolutely, that's interesting*. Long ago she dropped like a hot potato any terms which had the slightest whiff of jargon, such as *transference*, *projection* and *narcissism*. Along with *ergo* and *closure* she left them for the amateurs, as she put it, the "pop-psychologists."

Now she turned to Erica quite softly. "What is it about my father? I'd like you to tell me. I suppose he made the move, though you can't be entirely Miss Innocent. I know him better than you. I should tell you he's incorrigible. When he plays around with a woman it's all about him. His pathology is that of an obsessive. Of course I love him dearly. You do know that. For as long as I can remember he's had his little flings. Saddled with my stepmother, who can blame him? Do you have the right time? Thank you. In point of fact, it's more biological than psychological. One is the dominant aspect. This has changed our relationship to each other. That's only natural. Since when is it you've been seeing each other? I don't know why you should do this!"

She was just getting started.

"Not now," Erica said, and left the kitchen.

In the hall she turned and bumped into Lindsey.

"Are you all right?"

"What does it look like?" Erica felt like saying. In her room she closed the door.

To think that a few days in such a place of unimaginable stillness could produce disorder, uncertainty, impatience, difficulties with herself and those around her. Erica did not usually exhibit signs of restlessness, and she knew it.

If philosophy had any use it would calm her down. It had on other occasions. She would go back to the Greeks, possibly the Germans. Her toe-in-the-water theories on Time were not applicable here.

She would have a shower.

By being decisive Erica returned to something approaching her normal self. And once under the steaming water she began to see and even to feel that the clearness and firmness, which had taken her so far, had made her unattractive—muscular. A matter of changing a bit. And as she soaped her chest she saw Sophie's father, Harold, warts-and-all. She gave a private smile. Harold Perloff who had shown a true interest in her. Erica wanted to hear the voice of experience, deep and measured. She could listen to it all day. Sitting on her sofa he draped a hand over her shoulder. She liked that. And then as she dried herself with the large towel she considered for a moment Roger. With him, she realized she waited and wondered what he would come out with next— an unusual man. She couldn't quite believe he'd want to go into town with Sophie.

Lindsey glanced up from the table when Erica stepped into the kitchen.

"Do you mind if I use the telephone? Things are getting complicated, and I dislike complications."

Lindsey looked interested.

The phone was near the door. Resting the receiver on her shoulder, Erica ran her eyes over the locally printed business cards pinned to a board on the wall. These were for shearing contractors, fertilizer people, bore-sinkers, pump and tank specialists, seed merchants, stock and station agents—a pattern of experience, of thoughts put into practice. Such activities went ahead, unknown to the city.

"It's me—speaking from back of beyond. I wanted to hear how you were."

Lindsey got up to go, but Erica shook her head. She didn't mind who listened.

"I'm not sure when I'll be back. There's more to this than I imagined. There are many pages to look at. Some of it could be interesting. The homestead, it has those wide verandas. There are flocks of sheep. My ambition is to see a fox."

Nodding, Erica gave a laugh. "I'll be careful of snakes and other temptations." She whispered something into the phone, then paused.

"You didn't tell me that. When is this happening? I can't say when I'll be coming back. I'd like to, yes. I'm sorry, things are difficult here. Has Sophie spoken to you?"

When Erica sat down without speaking, Lindsey said, "What I would suggest—"

"My head examined is what I need."

"I was thinking would you like a cup of tea?"

The modesty of it made Erica smile.

"Thank you for this," she said.

"It's what we do here. If there's some sort of difficulty, or if it rains, or someone's had a baby—or when there's nothing happening at all—we tend to head for the teapot."

Erica only half-listened. She was wondering what it was that made Sophie turn her attention to Roger.

"But I believe coffee has taken over Sydney. I can't see it happening here."

Together they peeled the potatoes and shelled the peas.

It became dark as Lindsey told of her long friendship with a neighbor. And it was as if she was talking to herself. "We just clicked," came her explanation. "And it wasn't as if he was unhappy in his marriage. I knew Lorraine, I was her friend." Three years ago this month he died in one of those ludicrous agricultural accidents. He was a strong man, early forties. A branch from a Brittle Gum fell on him as he drove a tractor underneath. Waiting in her usual spot she saw it happen.

Erica began looking at her. This would explain her immobility.

"It was a terrible time. Everybody knew. I thought I was going to go mad. I couldn't sleep. Wesley was here. I thought I was stronger than I was. I still haven't got over it. I keep thinking about him—and he's simply not here. For two years I went to a psychologist, whatever they're called. Once a week I stayed overnight in Sydney. He didn't want to know about the accident, he wanted to go way back. I took a dislike to him. He had awful ginger hair."

Erica sat listening. "I haven't had what has happened to you. I was young when my father died. You will never get over it. It is now a part of you."

Out of sympathy, Erica began telling her about Harold, without revealing he was Sophie's father. Almost old enough to be her own father. Therefore he was a solid figure of a man, crammed with knowledge he didn't bother letting out, all sorts of stuff, and with experience, difficult European experience. He was in business, a manufacturer. They could only manage to see each other every few weeks. It had been going on for almost a year now. Erica heard herself talking rapidly.

Lindsey nodded. It only reminded her of the nearby one she no longer had.

After a while she asked, "Do you think something worthwhile can be found in Wesley's papers? Roger and I would like to think so." She glanced at the clock on the wall. "Where *are* those two? They might have gone rabbit shooting. Just joking! It's what the young men do for fun around here, except no one's exactly saying Roger's young."

At eight o'clock Erica and Lindsey tucked into the roast which was by then overdone, and a fine bottle of South Australian shiraz. Lindsey found some cigarettes. They washed the dishes, and left the table set for two. Forgetting the idea of coffee they vowed to continue their conversation at breakfast, that is, their friendship, as only two women know how.

25

AND JUST as the major and minor religions have their disciples who can quote chapter and verse, and are determined to hold on to and hold aloft the core of the thing, there on the page, to suffer no deviance, often with formidable learning and courtesy, and others impatient, cold, "brooking no argument," so too psychoanalysis has its disciples anxious to preserve its fundamentals, the way the original measurement of the meter is displayed in a glass case (somewhere in Paris). Much energy and refinement are spent correcting, or bringing back into the fold, heretics who veer off to form alternative schools, alternative readings, seen as interesting, certainly, but a watering-down or misinterpretation, at worst a travesty of the basic tenets; and as a consequence there have been scuffles, threats, committee-coups, proselytizing publications and lawsuits throughout Europe and North America, in turn producing various forms of psychological stress, some of which require treatment. Where more and more followers become involved, the purity of an idea is hard to preserve.

One difficulty is psychoanalysis cannot be "proven," something a number of philosophers have pointed to. Meanwhile, those in analysis continue to attend their twice or more weekly sessions unaware of the turmoil at the center. After all, what is of concern to them is the Self.

Other movements such as Surrealism back in the nineteen-twenties have had their purges. Those who didn't fit or follow the Manifesto were turfed out without ceremony. Another place to look are political movements, Marxism above all, the feminist movement more recently, or sporting associations, university departments, where rebels or independent thinkers have been ostracized, expelled, and in many cases exterminated (not in the feminist movement or sporting associations).

Beware of women who are or have been in analysis, even if only for a year or two. Surrendering themselves to a most intimate and self-revealing way of thinking aloud, of allowing layers to be lifted in order to reach and recognize the difficult Self, afterwards recognizing the strange sense of well-being, of achievement even, as if cleansed, or beginning to be cleansed—lightened—can produce a quiet condescension towards anyone else who hasn't undergone the same treatment (you would have no idea how hard work it is, and the layered benefits, the glimpse of clarity). Time spent in analysis is more intimate than believing in a religion; virtually no condescension quiet or otherwise is to be found amongst religious converts. Tread warily with those who have sisters in analysis or the earnest sister practicing as an analyst in Chicago or Manhattan, Newcastle or Sydney, and who attends conferences elsewhere, for this filial connection exerts a double anxiety, double loyalty, on the already committed remaining sister. It can be seen to produce further competitive confusion between them, or a bristling defense against nonbelievers, occasionally obscured by a jokey manner to the subject in general, or rather, their own adoption of psychoanalysis in particular. Interesting, when one sister goes into therapy the other sisters often follow.

26

AGAIN, ERICA was woken early. Imagine her dismay when she arrived in the kitchen to find the two places still set, and on the stove the peas and potatoes cold in their saucepans. Either Roger Antill and Sophie had stumbled in so late they didn't feel like eating, or they hadn't yet come back (from where?). Quickly she made some toast. She had trouble swallowing. It was behavior typical of Sophie. Where two people are thrown together in travel, small annoyances grow into unbearable personality disorders.

In the shed all was quiet, in shadow. Erica took a deep breath. She picked up the ruined pages and placed them to one side on the floor. She arranged the desk. Papers everywhere. Sitting in the philosopher's chair she assumed a look of concentrated determination as she reached for a pile and began reading. Some pages consisted of nothing but a single sentence. When any of these statements stopped her in her tracks Erica marked them. Other pages were filled with Wesley's hectic blue handwriting. Here and there sentences and entire paragraphs were crossed out. "Pig-headed" was a word she saw, but couldn't find again. After several hours a thread, or a suggestion of a thread, a story-journey, emerged. Then it petered out; it appeared to stop altogether. Later it would start up again.

What had gone on in this man's life? He seemed to be tearing his hair out. More than most he suffered from the common intrusions of everyday life.

He also revealed an anxiety towards time.

Taking a breather, Erica went to the window and surveyed the bare ground. She tried to picture it before the single-minded philosopher cut the trees down, a grove of slender gums, strips of bark on the ground, the usual Australian mess. What extremes people take to gain clarity.

Erica went back to reading.

At ten o'clock, Sophie clattered in. Immediately the corrugated shed echoed another woman's restlessness.

Without turning Erica said, "Try not to spill anything on these pages, please."

"I'm going back to Sydney. I'd like to leave this morning, if possible."

Erica glanced up. Without noticing, Sophie had her feet on some of the pages.

"It doesn't look as if you've had much sleep."

"I've made a decision."

Noticing Erica's frown, she hurried on. "I've just been talking to him. I've gone through the issues." As Sophie began pacing, Erica wondered who she could be talking about. "The wife is an irrelevance. She does him no good. My idea is that he becomes one of my clients. I consider that a brainwave. I would see him regularly. Which is why I want to leave immediately, but of course there's no train."

Erica couldn't help her. "Look at all this. There's three or four days' solid reading, at least."

"What I was thinking was, there's your car. If it's not being used."

Erica looked at her. Loosely draped around her throat was the scarf from last night. Erica glanced at the pages waiting to be appraised. She could feel the task becoming interesting. It was like panning for gold. Framed by the window was a small part of the sky. Everything was closer to silence here. The sunset last night! And tonight Erica looked forward to a repeat, the sky down the end screaming out heat and immensity, the great cycle of day turning into night, cockatoo-gray feathery, and pink-tinted, until gradually, then suddenly, closing down. She wondered whether Lindsey might be a drinker. And what was Roger—Mr. Roger Antill, if you please—going to say about Sophie leaving?

"Do be careful," she handed Sophie the keys. "That's seven hours on that road by yourself. Are you sure you should be doing this?"

At the door Sophie paused, "You didn't ask about last night. He spent practically the whole evening wanting to know about you. How had you become an 'expert'? I told him the most lurid things I could think of, and more."

Below the steps Erica stood alongside Lindsey, and like a pair of Adelaide aunts they waved as Sophie drove away.

"I didn't really get to know her," Lindsey said.

"Does Roger know she's gone?"

"Most of the time I don't know what my brother's up to."

Without Sophie already the house felt settled. Lindsey made tea and took it out onto the veranda.

"Now that Sophie's not here I feel I can have some cake. She must do exercises, and things like that. She looks good in her clothes."

"Sophie is a formidable shopper." Not wanting to sound as if she was sticking sharp knives into her friend, Erica added thoughtfully, "Her father always encourages Sophie, though Sophie doesn't always think so."

"I can just see her being good at her work."

Lindsey went on, "When I think of Wesley, I realize he had mini-breakdowns of some kind. I meant to ask Sophie for her expert's opinion. He'd be going along all right, cheery enough, then he'd spend a week locked in his room. Until I got used to it, I'd knock on his door. There'd be no answer. I'd leave his dinner on a tray outside. After a few days he'd appear, and it was as if nothing happened."

It was time for Erica to return to the shed, to submerge herself in the pages. But it was comfortable on the veranda, in the cane chairs with cushions, looking out past the sheds to the brown-purple horizon, tall spreading gum on the left. Lindsey was easy company. The way she allowed, and even encouraged gaps, imitated the landscape.

"Both my brothers I would put in the unusual category," she now said. "But then I suppose I'm biased. Wesley was single-minded. You've no doubt noticed. He had our father's jaw. Because of his work, Wesley had very orderly, methodical habits. It almost made him an unpleasant brother. Every other day he had to have boiled eggs." Lindsey turned to Erica. "Do you know he asked for his rain gauge to be buried with him? Can you believe it? Of course Roger carried out his wishes."

Wesley used to go down with the proverbial splitting headache. No amount of darkened room and Aspro would ease it. They were aftershocks, not necessarily to do with the way he applied his mind to the most impossible of subjects—but then unremitting hard thinking each and every day of the week, from the moment he woke up, was bound to have an effect, upsetting the brain cells even. Often Lindsey came upon him with his hand covering his eyes. He was one of those hungry dogs with a bone, he said to his sister. "There's nothing I can do about it, nothing at all."

Apparently Roger had his oddities too. Nothing serious — but she didn't want to go into them.

Amongst Erica's strengths was an ability to concentrate. All Erica had to do was rest her elbows on a desk, and squash her face in her hands, and look down at a page. For hours at a time Erica could work in that position. Concentrating, she hardened. It was something she was aware of.

Now having skipped lunch she stopped reading to lean back in the chair. Sophie was driving back to Sydney in the small car, music station playing loudly. Couldn't she see that the long solitary drive, a mad dash back, was not going to lead to anything? It was as if she was rushing into a future with sun in her eyes.

Erica stood up and stretched.

She went outside.

Instead of this time walking from the homestead on the right side she took the left side, and walked down and further across and further along until there were no more gates. It became progressively rougher, mallees and scraggy gums, just an occasional animal track. The land also fell away behind her. If she turned and had seen the lack of signs she might have paused. It was while walking that Erica decided to build, definitely, on her strengths, which seemed to be clearness in thought, a dispassionate logic before a given situation, an expressionless firmness, even a bit of coolness — or, all those strengths, while somehow avoiding the coolness.

It would help in the appraisal of Wesley Antill's papers, and when the task was finished (concluded) strengthen her own philosophical work, her own papers, as well as keep on even keel the personal aspects of her life. It was while thinking along these lines, and glancing at birds and stopping to look at ants, that somehow Erica lost her sunglasses. One moment she was wearing them, next she had nothing.

As she searched she cursed and wished she had someone alongside to help. She moved around in circles, searching low branches, under bushes, on bare ground. For this to have happened she must have been wandering in a dream. She even began to doubt she had been wearing them at all.

When she turned to go back she didn't recognize anything. She kept walking in the direction she imagined the homestead to be. She also wanted more open ground—away from the dry bushes. Another reason for walking was to avoid getting cold. It was past four o'clock. All Erica had on was a short-sleeve cotton shirt, stopping short at the hips. Keep on walking just a little longer until she met a fence; a fence—any post with wire—would lead to the house.

Less than ten paces away Erica saw the beer-colored fur move. It was behind some grass. The fox remained side on, then walked away, stopping and looking back at Erica, who had frozen, before it disappeared.

The ground now leveled out, but still no fences.

In the space of a few days so many things had happened. Now this. It was not yet panic stations, but she had to be careful. She sat on a very large rock—"to gather her thoughts," a phrase she had always liked. She was lost, but not really lost. It would soon be dark. What if it started snowing? Be like the fox—*fit in, be unafraid*. And her small face assumed the expression of looking ahead, determined, clear, set.

Still she remained in the one spot.

At first the sound coming from somewhere was so unexpected Erica barely noticed. Only as it came closer and an unhurried bumping and rattling took over, which became altogether louder and intrusive, did Erica stand up.

Any relief she felt seeing the familiar truck made her annoyed at herself.

"Are you coming with me, or do you want to freeze to death?"

Once she was seated, Roger Antill looked at her. He took off his coat.

"Thank you," Erica said. Heavy, and far too large, it smelt of sheep, soil and wheat dust.

"It suits you."

Driving one-handed he went in the opposite direction to where she had been heading.

"If it's Sydney you were looking for, it's that-a-way."

"I'm not in the business of following Sophie."

"Sophie. What's she been up to?"

Erica explained why Sophie had rushed back to Sydney—for no good reason, in her humble opinion. We are talking here about a married man who has a wife. Sophie had never given a full description of him.

Roger didn't have a lot to say about this, and as Erica, feeling comfortable in the cabin in his warm coat, went on critical of Sophie and her impulses, he said, "Is she keen on him, or not?" It was sometimes difficult, Erica explained, to tell the difference between Sophie's restlessness and her sudden interest in another person, a man especially. Roger nodded.

So they drove and Erica waited as he stopped and checked a few things, such as stray ewes and the floats in the water troughs. Everything threw a long shadow; then it was dark.

"Anyway," he said accelerating up to the lighted house, "it looks as if you're marooned here, on this place."

"Marooned?" That was funny. "I don't think I've ever been marooned before in my life."

And to Lindsey in the welcome of the kitchen he reported, "I've saved her from the crows and the ants. She would have been picked clean inside a week."

Lindsey saw Erica in her brother's coat. "I, of course, assumed you were working in the shed."

"Just a walk," Erica shrugged, "that took longer than expected."

"Down past the long paddock," Roger said in a low voice.

"See if there's a special bottle left in our father's cellar."

After a two-course meal and one glass too many, and if the hands were past ten, Erica normally would be feeling drowsy. She would be thinking about the next day. But circumstances were not normal. She had survived an adventure, just. She had been saved by him. Here he was seated next to her. A very strange sensation, one she had not experienced before. She was grateful to him for coming by chance upon her, and then to treat it all lightly. Otherwise, she would still be out there, by herself, freezing to death. No wonder she felt light-headed, more talkative than usual. And it was why she followed him out onto the veranda on his suggestion, instead of hesitating or saying no thank you very much, her usual automatic response. Be unafraid. Why not? Besides, he leapt to his feet to find a coat, this time a heavy greatcoat—the sort that used to feature in Army Disposal stores—and smelling of sheep, but also metal, engine oil, poultry—not unpleasant, not at all—which he draped ceremonially over her. She could recline in the deck chair, a philosopher at rest, except for one leg hanging over. "It's too cold out here," Lindsey said. "I'll leave you to it." Through the kitchen window Erica glimpsed her taking a swig straight from the bottle (and didn't feel surprised or saddened).

To her left he cleared his throat.

"Philosophy is your expertise. So what have you figured out for yourself?"

"I am still working on it. Working through it." This may have sounded precious, so she added, "I don't like the word 'philosophy' anymore. It sounds a bit off-putting, doesn't it?"

Whatever she said out there on the veranda was sounding dry, theoretical, tentative, *small*, and her "philosophy" was all of those things, of little use for the complexities of living.

While listening, Roger Antill hadn't moved.

Erica felt a pleasant warmth through her hands, face and legs.

"As far as I can see, your brother was constructing a theory of the emotions."

"What's that, based on personal experience?"

"I suppose, in part. Whoops! Sorry." Her left foot touched his. What an idiot: he'd think she was—

"All I know," Roger from the left, "is when our brother returned here, and he stood outside looking at the view, I said to Lindsey, 'He's gone all white in the hair department, and he's not much older than me.'"

"This can happen," Erica nodded from her chair. The difficulty was knowing how to live in reaction to others.

"I don't know why our brother became like he did. Sophie might be able to throw light on that one."

"She must be in Sydney by now."

She wondered if Roger was at all like his brother; did they even look similar? Was Wesley a helpful man?

Erica touched his arm. "I hope today you hadn't gone out specially looking for me. If you hadn't found me, I'd be in a sorry state by now."

"I'd be driving around all night sounding the horn, letting off firecrackers. I'd be organizing search parties, hundreds of men beating the bushes with sticks. Helicopters using searchlights. We would have found you. You might have ended up a bit worse for wear, that's all."

It was the general immensity she was no longer afraid of. "Overarching," a word she had used in her philosophical work before.

When he asked how long it would take to finish the appraisal, Erica looked straight ahead and answered, "Many months, at least. Possibly more."

In the dark alongside came an exaggerated groan.

She gave him a push. "You should be pleased to have a guest, and one who doesn't give the slightest bit of trouble."

"I could do with a philosophy for myself. Nothing fancy." He stood up. "You must be getting cold." Taking her hand he raised her from the deck chair. Taller than her, he let his hand settle on her hip. It didn't go away. But it seemed he was thinking of something else. She couldn't see his face.

Erica reached up. "Thank you for today."

She didn't know whether it was relief, gratitude or carelessness. One of philosophy's functions has always been to shine light into the dimly lit, the imprecise, the hopeful.

As Roger walked to the door he kept his arm around her waist. In the kitchen she took off and handed him the greatcoat and stood there the way she would remove for him a gown of some sort, a bathrobe.

27

——NATURALLY, I assumed—took for granted—could not think otherwise (I hadn't thought about it enough)—that Cynthia, laden down with the embarrassment of her cameras, would come with me to the adjoining country, Germany. I didn't let on it would be on my way home.

It was unthinkable that I would not include Germany. My studies in Sydney, and wanderings in England and Europe to establish some sort of deep-footing in philosophy, would not have culminated; I would have demonstrated, if only to myself, a *lightness* towards the subject. Never has there been so much dilettantism as today! Everywhere I look. The various recent *isms* have seen to it. After Greece—I had decided not to set foot in Athens— Germany is the natural home for philosophy. It is hardly worth stating.

Germany has given us not one or two, but five of the giants in Western philosophy.

"It must be something in the water," was George Kybybolite's explanation. Or was it his brother, Carl, trying to make light of it?

Although it was high time I returned home, I toyed with the idea of learning German.

I told all this to Cynthia who had her camera resting on her thigh. We were in a beer cellar, near the station. She seemed to be only half-listening. I took it to be an obvious acceptance of the invitation—why would you even bother asking, et cetera? By train we would slowly zigzag via Hanover, Leipzig and other important centers, to Berlin. I began to anticipate my entry into Germany as a kind of smothering newsreel-dark greenness.

Raising the camera and focusing on nothing in particular Cynthia told me she was going off to Vienna with one of the Kybybolite brothers, George. They were leaving in the morning.

It had been going on under my nose!

As she kept her camera to her eye panning along the patrons of the beer cellar, I didn't know what to say.

I must admit my relaxed attitude to the present—to myself and those around me—and to things like the taste of beer—was blown to pieces. Suffering a rejection hadn't happened to me before. As an attempt at justification I told myself I didn't really know Cynthia, because there was not a lot to know. She was at least fifteen years younger than me. If we talked she seemed to be somewhere else. Although we had been eating and sleeping together for barely a month or so, I wondered if I had mistreated her. (Answer was: how?) I sat very still and imagined how I must appear to her. But my abruptly altered view of her made this difficult. In her eyes I was a man, but one of the solemn ones. The marble brow, constantly trying to make sense—not far from coming across as a pedant. Boring! Meanwhile, the loud Kybybolite brothers in their democratic shirts and lumberjack boots went on horsing around, cracking jokes, "good company."

A slender black-haired woman who only occasionally smiled. She gave me the flick.

The narrowness of my way of thinking had undoubtedly infected my behavior. It had always carried the danger of rejection. Otherwise, no matter how carefully I examine my feelings, I do not get very far. I can never understand myself, not completely. Show me somebody who does. (And what does this mean?)

——BY THE TIME I crossed the border and entered Germany my thoughts had returned to where they should have been in the first place. Journeys by train tend to direct me towards extra-thinking. I've noticed this before. In England I became addicted to train travel—something to do with being a passenger through time, where the fleeting present can be seen instantly becoming the past, while the future goes on, perpetually out of reach? Some of my best thinking was done on trains going up and down the British Isles, just as my best note-taking took place in railway hotels, on railway platforms, and in the cafeterias.

I shared a table in the dining car with a completely bald picture-framer and his smaller friend who made violins, both from Mittenwald. Already seated was a man missing an arm, who said nothing. When I gesticulated to help him cut his frankfurt into pieces he got up and moved away. I assumed he'd lost an arm in the war. The two old friends from Mittenwald laughed their heads off. "Anybody who has a cough has tuberculosis," one nodded to the other. Fair enough.

The German fields, as they were called, possess a many-layered heaviness, like an ordered bog, and in the hamlets and towns the German churches strive to rise above them, using geometry, decoration, music.

It was the picture-framer, I believe, who said that everything in the world ended up, in one way or another, being framed—"contained" was his term. A face being the obvious, everyday example. It is framed by hair. And the human body. It is contained by clothing chosen to emphasize or subdue certain features. Things at one remove from the truth, such as oil paintings of fields, or of apples and grapes on a table, are given assistance by a frame which increases the illusion. This was said in heavy pidgin-English. Here the violin-maker quoted from somebody, "there's no such thing as an ugly bridge," though since we were at that moment not crossing a river I assumed it had to do with violins. Odd how I remember the young woman, English, I found myself sitting alongside under a tree in Hyde Park, who had a violin case and proceeded to eat a vegetarian salad. Unusual eyes—set wide apart. She was on her way to a violin class. As we sat with our backs against the tree I imagined—without meaning to—her standing upright, practicing Bartok or something difficult, naked. In an unaffected way she told me her father had been a mushroom farmer. She loved mushrooms. Every day, she said, she cooked and ate mushrooms.

We bump into a stranger, and soon forget about them; while others—there is no logic—we find ourselves remembering.

The two craftsmen from Mittenwald shared a serene manner. As we talked they kept glancing at the passing landscape framed by the large window, accustomed to their land, while taking note of it.

When they left the train at Heidelberg they bowed after a fashion and didn't wave from the platform. No, I didn't get their names.

Alone in the dining car I wrote to Rosie, describing them, and in a burst of irritation claimed I would never have met such interesting types, let alone their conversation, if I hadn't been on a train in southern Germany. And in a further burst of what I can only think was a convoluted form of homesickness asked if there was a single violin-maker in the city of Sydney.

I went further, "Have you thought about making a visit? If not, why not?"

Instead of returning home I was suggesting Rosie drop everything and join me in Germany.

I wrote again.

I followed with a postcard, "I'd like you to be here now." I emphasized, "If you see what I mean."

To Lindsey I explained I was on my way home, at least heading in the right direction. First, I had to finish a bit of research ("the special atmospherics"). I gave a description of the middle-aged German women having lunch in restaurants who have this habit of wearing hats as they wield their knife and fork, huntsmen-looking hats, often with a tall feather. It looked as if it was about to snow. And, because my brother would read it, I listed the crops I had managed to identify in passing.

——AT A PLACE CALLED BURETEN as I walked along a path strewn with leaves I paused. I took a few more steps, then I stood still. It was something the violin-maker had said, a quote or more likely a misquote—people giving a quote invariably get it wrong—which his friend, the bald picture-framer, translated for me, although it was not from any philosopher I knew. He said, "Without moving a centimeter, one can know the whole world." And I recalled then the picture-framer telling me his friend had never stepped foot outside Germany. In fact, he only rarely left his house on the edge of Mittenwald, which doubled as his workshop, mostly to enter a nearby forest to select a spruce or a maple to be cut down for his violins.

The most ordinary and unoriginal ideas can stop us in our tracks.

When a glimmer of clarity comes into view it is like a sliver of diminishing light, and it is essential to stop everything, stay still, be patient, in order to continue "seeing" it. Nothing moved in amongst the trees. At that moment I realized there was no reason to be on a path in a forest somewhere in the middle of Germany, and that all of my deliberate and lengthy wanderings had been a waste of time, an indulgence, an example of evasion. "The further one goes, the less one knows" I have written in my notebook. I had picked it up from somewhere. Normally I steer clear of the Delphic utterance. It was more a matter of returning home, back to the old homestead (those enormous skies), staying in the one spot, staying put. Without moving a centimeter I would come to regard my own self as a place to travel through, slowly, and, in an interested manner, *examine*, and through myself and myself alone attempt an explanation of the broader world. I'd be better off.

And no longer traveling I also took to mean not studying the works of others. At home on the land I had seen with my own eyes hybrid ewes and calves—misfittings, mismatchings, *mistakes, errors of nature*—animals struggling with five legs or three, pink eyes, and so on. Our father told us of a lamb born in the district with two heads. These aberrations were discussed in front of our mother at the dinner table.

Hybrid creations are not singular; they do not last.

I remained standing on the path, still not moving, until the weather turned nasty.

There and then I should have phoned Rosie saying, "Listen, stop! There's no point in coming here. I'm coming home."

Aside from wanting to see Rosie, and be comforted by her, I had the idea of showing her my progress, how I had changed, I mean how I had improved, how I had become wiser. I realized I shouldn't be there, not in Germany, I had nothing to show for my years away, nothing in me had any substance; Rosie would quickly see this.

But I had already phoned her. "I have been waiting to hear your voice," she said. We spoke for an hour, easy and intimate, and she agreed to come. She was on her way.

——Rosie stayed with me in Germany less than five weeks.

I met her in Berlin and wore new cords and a heavy brown coat to the knees. The cheap trousers, old shirt and boots were out of the question. I had also shaved.

As Rosie entered the terminal I saw she had on just a thin cardigan. Didn't she know it was winter in Europe? It irritated me—her provincialism. I immediately put my new coat onto her shoulders. After buying some gloves we took a walk in the Tiergarten.

We hadn't seen each other for—I had lost count. Rosie was thirty-two. She still lived in the same apartment on Macleay Street. Why hadn't she married? (Maybe she had.) How would we go on speaking again? Above all—I remembered—back in Sydney her easy acceptance of everything that came towards her. In that sense a modern woman. Over the five or six years her face had become more complex. And larger hips—pensive voluptuous woman. I hired a little car. Taking our time we drove from one place to another, Leipzig, Freiberg and the inevitable hotel over a water-wheel.

Rosie wasn't interested in museums. Cathedrals she had to be dragged into. The castles on the Rhine left her absolutely cold. Instead of tramping the cities she preferred the towns and hamlets, as they are called, and in our overheated rooms she lay on the bed or sofa offering her raised hip, reading, sometimes topless. I noticed her looking at me. I had forgotten how little Rosie spoke. And now in Germany she seemed to speak even less.

I had the feeling Rosie was on the verge of telling me something. She seemed to be measuring my reactions.

She believed we had all the time in the world.

Of the eleven notebooks, nine of them I threw away at Bureten. Before I had second thoughts I chucked the rest.

They say the philosopher must set an example, if only to himself.

I started a new notebook.

Isn't it a matter of putting both hands over the eyes, then after a while removing them?

——IT WAS NEAR TO—hardly matters where—within earshot of another river—early afternoon. Rosie was driving. A mass of blackness flowed out from the floor of the forest, and within the branches and leaves too, and the river was black or at least very dark, I'll always remember that. The road was about the same width as the river, and a

similar glossy blackness, which gave the appearance of a
river drained of water alongside the real river. The clouds
and sky itself were dark. It was about to snow. A hare ran
across the road. With my rural background I could explain to Rosie the difference between it and the common
rabbit.

Rosie and I had settled into an easy intimacy. From the
first day in Berlin we slept together. Now as she drove I removed my hand from between her legs and pointed to the
restaurant. It had a glassed-in terrace jutting over the river.
In the midst of darkness the glaring white of the tablecloths
had caught my eye.

Because Rosie was happy, I felt happier—by that I mean,
carefree.

The temptation is to think and write vaguely, anything
to avoid the difficulty of precision.

Although we were warm enough, I ordered cognacs.

Thought can only exist parallel to nature.

"I think I shall have," she put on a *la di da* voice, "some
river fish."

When she felt like it Rosie could be funny. Now she had
a relaxed bright-eyed look.

Except for an elderly couple further along, the rest of
the tables were empty. Light snow began floating down.
There we were, in the warm restaurant, looking through
the window at it.

"Have a gander at the waiter's ears, how big they are."

Rosie turned. The waiter also had small eyes.

"I'm sure I've seen him in a film somewhere." She frowned for a second, then shrugged.

As I looked at her, I smiled.

For no apparent reason she said, "I feel completely safe here."

It was another way of expressing contentment.

"And it might amaze you to know, since you think you know everything, that I'm mad about all this snow. You don't believe me?"

"The first time I saw you was on the roof in a bikini, covered in suntan oil. It's not a sight I'd forget in a hurry."

"Thank you very much."

It was that sort of conversation.

After the bottle of Moselle we selected pastries. I ordered a cognac, then another. At this point, Rosie who had been talking freely became pensive. The snow continued to fill in the hollows on the other side of the river. When considering the cold regions of the earth I wonder what we are doing there. How we manage to survive. The importance in the harsh environment of the family—"the family-unit," I said aloud.

"You must admit it's pretty nice here."

"Why 'must admit'?" she asked.

I'd thrown out the old notebooks with their dodgy propositions and dependence on other thinkers. Because I was beginning anew I felt fresh. I was keen. Rosie was with me. And the snow had transformed the river scene outside into one found on picture postcards.

It was then that I decided to say I was thinking of returning to Australia within weeks, and not taking my eyes off her asked if she would join me on the property.

"I've only just arrived!"

This was Rosie avoiding commitment by being light-hearted. If I waited she would do a switch into seriousness.

"What would I do all day? The answer is yes."

Returning to the car she spoke in a way I had not heard before. "I was expecting you to write to me when you left Sydney. I don't know why you didn't. All I knew was that you were in London. Is that a big city, or is that a big city? I didn't know what to do. I had to get in touch, which I did through Lindsey. I introduced myself. I like your sister. Anyway, I received—finally—a card. It had a London policeman on the front."

She reversed out onto the road.

"You just seemed to bolt. I couldn't understand, I still don't. It was as if you wanted to forget our situation. Remember how we were? You once told me the word 'natural' is not possible. I thought we were natural together."

The dark road followed the river. I just put my hand between her legs, where I knew it was as dark and alive as the river.

"I can well understand you wanting to shoot through from the ghastly Mrs. What's-her-face—the Kentridge woman. There's a terrible piece of work. But it's not as if I'm a tarantula or anything."

I remember thinking that a life consists of curiosities

satisfied. Also that complexities increase when things are obscured.

Rosie kept talking, "You should know. I became pregnant, it was yours. If I'd managed to get you, what would you have done? There's a philosophical question for you! I was left to make the decision alone. I would have made it anyway. But it was sad. It's made me sad. I don't really know why I did it."

I reached across to switch on the lights. It would be better to slow down, the road being icy.

"What do your philosophers say about that one? No, oh! Shit!"

Often I see the car swinging into a slide, and crossing the road it slid still faster, a dog on lino. Rosie gave a gasp. The stone bridge blocked the view. We hit, the car tilted forward and went over, and over again. Really, the thing was like a mad smashing animal. I was facedown on the bank, my mouth filled with snow. The rented car upside-down floated away.

——IT WOULD BE BETTER if I reviewed my life as a series of incidents, of sobering alterations—along with the observations, speculations and corrections, snatches of what had gone on in my mind, *thought-thinking*, and a few notes on what I have learnt more from study than "life," even if I have trouble saying exactly what I have learnt. A certain doggedness—is it necessary? Make note of the acts of oafish ignorance, the examples of blindness . . . how I had spent too long on a certain way of life, or following a single line of thought. ("Tunnel vision.") The aims we set ourselves when young are still there but more and more out of reach. There would be a list of the good deeds and the bad deeds. Proper due can be given to my curiosity in general. Each entry need not be long. A single sentence should do it. One entry per page. These could be tossed up into the air and allowed to settle in any order, for they are random parts of a single life, mine. It is worth a try. For one thing it would avoid each small town and each and every river and sunset Rosie and I had seen in Germany; or the fact that my hair turned the color of snow on the riverbank in Germany, and from that same moment I was a different, an altered, person. Or, "After he recovered in a *pension* in Vence, where for months he lay in a shuttered room like a dog, he returned to Sydney alone on 5 July, 2001, on news of the death of his father."

28

WHAT ROGER ANTILL called his "philosophy" cannot be taken seriously. Unlike his brother he had not spent years in study or sustained thinking on the subject; aside from Wesley's drafts in blue ink he had hardly read a single sentence on a philosophical subject. Roger was a plain-thinking pastoralist running thousands of acres of merino sheep. He had dirt under his fingernails. Even the way his "philosophy" came to him out of the blue has an amateur ring to it. Driving with Erica into town, Roger slowed and stopped in the shade under a tree. For a moment he rested his hands over the steering wheel and said nothing (gathering his thoughts). Dirt road, nobody for miles. With her big-city experience, Erica expected the sudden clammy-hand moment. He did—in an unexpected way. He reached across and took Erica's hand in order, he said, to demonstrate what he considered to be, not just a philosophy, a practical philosophy.

He had noticed that the hand, everybody's hand, followed the wishes of the mind, that is, thoughts, theories, moral positions, the passions, et cetera. The hand carries out the wishes of a decision; it is the practical rendition of a philosophy. The hand wields the sword, squeezes the trigger, does the strangling, signals the execution; both are raised in surrender. It waves goodbye. Any theory of the passions is eventually performed by the hand—hands and fingers wandering over the other body. How many bones in the hand? Twenty-seven. All at work in the service of a thought, a philosophical position. We shake hands. We work with our hands. Roger Antill didn't include agriculture, believing it is not philosophical enough. The pen is held in a hand. Philosophy depends for its creation on the hand. (Dreams and psychoanalysis do not!—Sophie.) Logic via medicine, the surgeon's hand. And music—the

composing and conducting of it, and the playing, or holding the microphone. How is the camera aimed, clicked or
rolled? Counting on fingers—I bet it was the source of
arithmetic. Signing of documents, applying to the face ideals of beauty; zipping up our bloody trousers. The hands of
the clock. Hands cut off as punishment.

Erica on the broad seat of the truck didn't know whether
to listen politely or laugh or nod encouragement—or come
in early, and demolish his idea, shoot it down in flames,
even if it was tentative, for this theory of hands, or whatever
it was, had no philosophical basis. It was little more than
detailing the obvious. (In Sophie's opinion, Roger's theory
revealed a condition of obsessive disorder. Please go find a
therapist, now.) But at the moment when Roger took her
hand, and she allowed it to rest in his, a small warm bird,
Erica, for all her training and devotion to logic, which over
time encouraged a certain severity, her remote and mascu-
line side, softened, and she proceeded to listen. He went
on listing examples of hand movements. She felt different.
Something was going on. And through the windscreen and
at the side remained the landscape, warm, golden and still,
which she hadn't until then seen before.

29

A PHILOSOPHER is a dissatisfied person.

Only small parts of the philosophical person are fully developed. A certain childishness.

"Why is there something rather than nothing?"

The puzzle is whether to continue with the *puzzle*. The puzzle? What are we doing *here*? What can be described. Et cetera. Life is the intruder on thought. The impossibility of being true, of being good, of not inflicting harm, or altering another person—while at the same time retaining and reinforcing individuality.

A study of ethics is more difficult than the emotions.

All is separate; everything is divided; separateness is the general condition.

Don't say "philosophy," say "provisional." A provisional philosophy, always provisional, a suggestion, nothing more.

I am incapable of distinguishing the truth. Nevertheless . . .

Philosophy is the modeling of imperfect materials.

The word *insofar*—attractive. To be used.

Sheep never stop their eating. The importance of leisure.

Philosophy doesn't "exist."

Work to one side of the conventional forms.

Terrain—useful word. The terrain of thinking, the shape of words.

The process of disturbing the mind is the mind.

There is nothing ordinary about any thing.

Philosophy as a natural force.

We end up becoming.

He picked up the word *overseeable*.

How to make anything of all the sensations.

The puzzle can never change: "How do I relate to the world and to that which I call my life?"
    Except it needs to be generalized.

Words are a recent addition to nature. A laconic culture is little more than one step above the oral culture.

Of course the philosopher can only despise photography. It is the enemy of philosophy, of what cannot be seen.

One emotion is replaced by another.

It has been said (Locke) that experience is like the furniture arriving in an empty house.
Because of the impossibility of living without experience, thoughts and ideas are not special in themselves.
From experience the emotions are activated.

The contest in the emotions between the cold and the warm. These are waverings of the mind.

Philosophy cannot exist without stubbornness.

"Modesty is a species of ambition."

Can there be such a thing as intellectual love?
Moral philosophy doesn't necessarily explain how we should live.
How is it possible to measure human thought against the fact, and the movement, of nature.

It was the surroundings, various bric-a-brac, appendages, attachments, not a commitment.

Is it anything more than self-absorption?

Why loyal to some, not to others?

"Without isolation there is nothing Noble or Lofty to be obtained."

Double, even triple, isolation. It begins to lead to indifference.

Ambition is the source of all emotions.

Many of the emotions are related to the past.

The desire to love is stronger than the desire to be loved.

Some emotions have no name.

Grief and melancholy are bodily functions. The woman weeps on a park bench. Love between two people is never equal. Love—a confusion. Loss is the greater one. We should never be surprised at our own emotions. Because of the emotions we can never really know the other person. We assume too much of ourselves and others. Memory— an interference. To let down, to be let down. Turning away.

Landscape and thought. It was cold in Germany. To be isolated and mind-cold.

By then I wanted, more than anything, numbness.

I may have had some sort of breakdown.

We are passive; only to a small extent can we be powerful.

How to remove subjectivity from *thought-thinking*.

The effort of moving towards a philosophy becomes itself the philosophy.

Love is a recognition of unbalanced affinities. See the uneven harmonies in nature.

"This creeping psychoanalysis of ordinary conduct."

The vague and undefined needs of one mean a reduction in the other.
   It is all given shape and described by words.

To live simply and quietly is almost a philosophy.

By keeping separate from people, I thought I could get on with my work.

We are philosophers; we cannot help being.